Illust

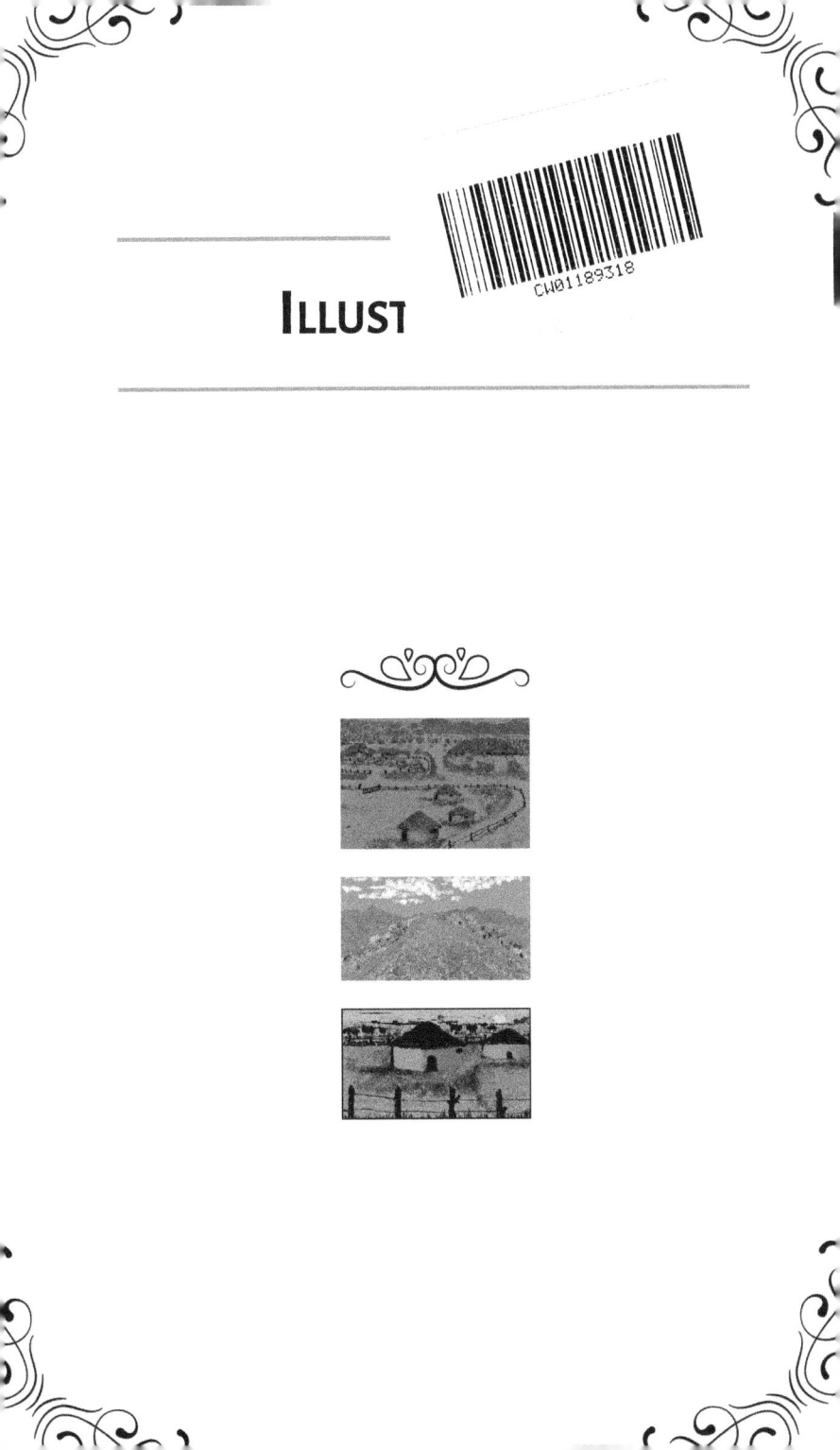

THE CLAIMANT AND THE EAGLE THAT FAILED TO SOAR

SekaBuhle gulps and looks at the brown bottle as if to say: how can I replenish you? How can I repay you for your sweet, soothing cascading into my belly? Without you social life is a joke dead and buried. How can I thank you for giving me so great a peace of mind in a world full of countless and unimaginable headaches and human indiscretions? You deserve my tender kisses and hugs every day. For whenever I pick up a calabash of you, I do not only drown my sorrows, sicknesses and silliness in there, I dance the break-dance of happiness, of togetherness, of peacefulness and fearlessness.

Beer, you bloody beat pork ten times.

The cocktail bar is abuzz with revelers and ladies of the night. Gestures, smiles and winks are not an uncommon way of communicating and interacting here. One can spot smart men in executive suits laughing as if they need to display a Learner sign on their lips because such laughter seems to veer off the road of good manners with a certain baffling measure of childishness and carefree. Some

A CURIOUS MOMENT

NDABA SIBANDA

PHOENIX VOICES PUBLISHING

Copyright © 2023 by Ndaba Sibanda

All rights reserved.

No part of this publication may be reproduced, stored or transmitted in any form or by any means, electronic, mechanical, photocopying, recording, scanning, or otherwise without written permission from the publisher. It is illegal to copy this book, post it to a website, or distribute it by any other means without permission.

This novel is entirely a work of fiction. The names, characters and incidents portrayed in it are the work of the author's imagination. Any resemblance to actual persons, living or dead, events or localities is entirely coincidental.

Ndaba Sibanda asserts the moral right to be identified as the author of this work.

Ndaba Sibanda has no responsibility for the persistence or accuracy of URLs for external or third-party Internet Websites referred to in this publication and does not guarantee that any content on such Websites is, or will remain, accurate or appropriate.

Designations used by companies to distinguish their products are often claimed as trademarks. All brand names and product names used in this book and on its cover are trade names, service marks, trademarks and registered trademarks of their respective owners. The publishers and the book are not associated with any product or vendor mentioned in this book. None of the companies referenced within the book have endorsed the book.

Contents

Foreword		1
Acknowledgement		2
Illustrations		3
1.	The Claimant And The Eagle That Failed To Soar	4
2.	The Immigrant With A Difference	46
3.	The Converse Holds True	66
4.	The Hen And The Cock	68
5.	Office Drama	78
6.	The Price of Perfidy And Pride	90
7.	A Speechless Assault Crime Story And Other Little Stories	103
8.	Why Standtoll And Trymore Collapsed	113
9.	Friendly Wars	114
10.	There Is A Method In Her Madness	116
11.	Something Gnaws	118

12.	The Pair Is Beyond Repair	129
13.	The Escape Route In The Dark	132
14.	Justice Denied	136
15.	The Inferno Of Madness	144
16.	The Five-Star Honeymoon Horror	153
17.	The Bambazonke Syndrome	161
18.	The Happy Headman's Dramatic Monologue	164
19.	Seeking Refuge	167
20.	No Exercise In Futility But The Future	169
21.	That Days General Knowledge Lesson	174
22.	For Everyday Life	178
23.	Wearing The Attire Of A Skunk	183
24.	Save Our Nation	190
25.	Roaring Into Bulawayo's Royal Treat	197
26.	About the Author	201

FOREWORD

Of the book, Alicia Guinot, *Europe Books*, declares:
Your work is one-of-a-kind, intriguing, and well-written; a fascinating piece with an unforeseen depth and the detailed manner in which you wrote, feels like we are watching a movie and bringing a whole world together.

Brenda Hale, President Phoenix Voices Publishing weighs in on this collection thus:

We received numerous submissions during our selection process, but your work truly stood out among the rest. Your exceptional storytelling, vivid characters, and compelling narrative captivated our team from the very first page. We believe that your book has the potential to make a significant impact on readers and contribute to the literary landscape in a remarkable way.

ACKNOWLEDGEMENT

Khumbulani Mleya - publicity officer for artists, a Host and Producer at Heart and Soul TV.

adult males are dancing a dance characterized by naughty bottoms that wiggle suggestively and shamelessly in the direction of the fairer sex.

A well-dressed man, possibly in his late eighties, is taking table manners to another level. A deplorable level for that matter. Not only is he using his unwashed fingers, fork and knife to air-lift chunks of food from his sizable and brimful plate, he is also bowing down his smallish and mainly whitehaired head, drawing out and dangling his tongue and lips like a dangerous serpent (and wait for this!) before scooping up mouthfuls of meat and rice. Yes, with his lolling tongue and drooping lips! At times, his sucking tongue has the liberty and nerve to let off some showers of saliva or to stray all the way to his girlfriend's plate and beer bottle. The young lady, who is certainly under age to be drinking in such a place, has perhaps been sneaked in after bribing the bar bouncers and authorities. Here the greasing of palms is more acceptable than mere verbal pleas. It is the norm. It is a normal abnormality. There is another dimension to it too. Here being a big party cardcarrying official has its unwritten and unlimited privileges and licenses. It can entitle one to change goal posts, to make lawful what is unlawful or the other way round, depending on which side one's sliced bread is buttered. One becomes law unto oneself. That is no issue at all. One is an untouchable and well-connected soul. That is what matters. It can also open doors and gates to everything, debauchery and corruption included.

She does not say it verbally: oh sugar daddy, your eating and drinking habits suck big time! Where is common sense in all this? The way she looks at him, doing all these antics says it

all. She is also thinking: the more I see him do this kind of nonsense, the lesser and lesser I think he's capable of doing other manly duties and responsibilities. Has he done noble deeds before? Mhmmm...How can a country prosper under such leaders? And is this his idea of being smart and romantic? Maybe he fantasizes living in the 1920s! What the heck did I get myself into here? He has been trying to smooch me in public but I've been ducking and dodging his cunning efforts. Trying what? My foot! Fancy him playing any game? Let us say I present him with a football pitch. I mean a penalty kick, to be more precise. Can he kick? What ball can he possibly play? Touch and sleep forever. Who gives a hoot anyway? Don't I come from a poverty-stricken child-headed family? He holds a big position in the so-called big party. At least I'll get a bit of his looted funds. There is no prize for disclosing how these chaps make money. The state of the economy bares it all. It says it all. It screams nothing else but drunkenness and weakness. Courtesy of the sickness and wickedness of the leaders who should be jealously guiding and nurturing it. For fun, I will look elsewhere. For the future, I will suck him to dryness and death and move forward.

Her elderly boyfriend is not discussing their future. Not today. He has not decided to turn back the hand of time and discuss life in the 1920s. He is not dwelling on politics either. He considers himself a modern fellow! "Innovation is my unwritten and unknown name. I love it. I live and lick it too", he utters in loud and steamy voice as if he he seeks to unleash and showcase his vocal and physical stamina. The pretty girlfriend stares at him with oh-really- you- fossilizedfoolingfoodie – type-of eyes. In his drunken state he thinks he is making a good impression. "We're living in the age of technology. What an exciting time to be alive and making use of new applications. For example, whenever I use touch screen technology, my fantasies become realities. I get transported to a world of fun and sophistication. My goodness, innovation is sophistication and sophistication is innovation. Now new finger control technology is out on the market. It'll blow your psyche up. It's so seamless you will think it's human. In fact it's smarter than human beings. Yes, you heard me right. Smarter! I've it as we speak. It doesn't require the screen to perform miracles and wonders. With this new technology people are able to kick a virtual soccer ball by moving or flicking their fingers. I can shift the hours on my clock by turning an imagined dial". The young lady is suppressing a giggle which is boiling and bursting to say: you don't get it old dude! That new technology won't make you perform miracles and wonders where it matters most— on the soccer pitch. It cannot and will not shift the hours on your clock and make you a young energetic boy again. Never. You're simply a touch-and -sleep player. A national liability too. Period.

Meanwhile a number of revelers are immersed in some bingo game, in bubble-gum love, yet others in chats that pass for shouts. They exhibit an amazing emotional ability and mobility to shift laughter to crying or crying to laughter in that order, and to their credit within a short space of time like some mourners at a funeral. One youthful charismatic church man is determined to pray and preach the gospel in the midst of such a jive of drunken dissonances and disturbances. Quoting a verse or two, he paces around the entire place, pleading with the beer drinkers to turn away from their drunken ways, and thirst and hunger not for the unsatisfying and worldly things. Sweating profusely, he invites them to soften their hearts and accept that they are lost and need to make a turnaround and lead a sanctified life. In that cacophony it is not amazing to discover that on the other hand, the revelers are also extending a hand of invitation to him. They want him to join their ranks."Hey man, slow down. You're obviously thirsty. Take a sweet sip and wash away your sweat. That is all I am asking of you. Please come over here?,"one beer drinker appeals to him. The young man of cloth says," come all all ye who are heavy -laden. Come and join me and you will never thirst again."One scantily dressed lady of the night winks at him before declaring,"Tonight is our delight. Tonight I shall join you in ways never known or seen or experienced before!"The manner her legs are freely spread out, one can be forgiven for concluding that she certainly has her mysterious ways of swallowing up her clients! Even with eyes closed, it is a scary sitting posture. If the eyes are bemoaning scary sights, the ears are not spared either. One couple seated near the doorway does not want to be outdone. It is singing with a discord of its life. What an orchestra! It is a hive of activity. The noise is bombarding the patrons' eardrums with a certain fury but not nobody seems to feel for them or feel it. It is show-time...

SekaBuhle in SiNdebele language means "the father of Buhle". Buhle means "Beauty". By the same token, NakaBuhle in SiNdebele means "the mother of Buhle." Parents in the Ndebele culture are usually called by the names of their first-born children. It is therefore important and advisable for first-born siblings to be exemplary in all aspects of life because of their bequeathed leadership role in the line of descent in particular and in society in general.

SekaBuhle has made up his mind and this is what he is imagining: I'll tell her in the face that there is only one bull which is supposed to bellow in that house. Me!   That's it!

Full stop! Period! It has to stop, this business of whimpering:

SekaBuhle, where have you been? Can't you see it's midnight? You're as drunk as a makorokoza (an illegal gold digger) who has struck gold! Why do you behave in an unsuitable fashion like an illegal gold panner? That's unacceptable. Appalling. I mean, your behavior leaves a lot to be desired. Behave in a dignified way please! You're an accountant for God's sake! I hate arguments and shouts. I'm not a fan of monitoring and controlling adults. Adults should behave responsibly.

But if adults fail to grow up or to outgrow foolish things, then there's a serious problem. It's even worse when someone's in denial! This makes me really sick. Baby-sitting an adult can never be fun!

I tried tell her that her daily preaching and accusations were not fun to me either. She shook me down to Mother Earth by commanding me to shut up. She said: please adhere to basic maxims of conversations like turn-taking. Now I am talking, do yourself a favor, listen. We can sing together at the same time, but we can't talk together at the same time. Be quiet for a while, is that too much to ask really? Don't say what you know or believe to be false. It's shameful! Do you have tangible evidence to support some of your lame excuses for coming home late? Be brief and relevant. And let your contribution to a discussion be informative. The beauty of a wife-husband interaction or any other form of communication is in the observance and submission to the cooperative principle. Communication is a two-way exchange of words."

I was pissed off. I could have swallowed a live chameleon there and then had it appeared. Where in the world have you heard this? In my culture this wildness is taboo. Not even a husband who has had overdoses of zwanamina ("taste me" or man-stupefying concoctions) would accept that arrogant behavior. No! His relatives would disown him on the spot! Not only that. They would dismiss him as dead! I, right in my mind, her one and only husband, supposedly-being sheepishly ordered to shut up while she talks, and talks nonsense for that matter! If communication is a two-way process, why is she the only one who wants to dominate? It's like she is that allknowing old-fashioned teacher who seeks to stand on a high platform in class to dish out her conveyor belt of incontestable knowledge, wisdom and instructions to the dull, obstinate and ignorant students. I see all the urge toward domination. I see all her contradictions. She had better castrate me first before l could become her acquiescent zombie.

How dare her! The one I paid handsome lobola (the bride price) for. Does she have a short memory or what? I will remind her that in a short and sharp manner that I can demand the return of all those ten fat cattle from babazala (father-in law). Please, she should not push her luck too far. A bombshell can implode in her hands. Yes, l can. After all, she has born me one child. Just one and imagine, Buhle is seven years now.

My wife has a disturbing habit. All she does is swallow. She keeps on swallowing up those maggot-like things from the clinic. And when I tell her: Thola, I want another child. Can't you see that Buhle is lonely and old? She has the nerve to tell me: Give me a break, Muzi, I'm on the pill. Please wake up from your Stone Age dream. I'm not a fan of beer-hall talk at all. Get this now. Let it sink into your head. I'm no childbearing machine for God's sake! Buhle has many companions in the neighborhood. She has good playmates. Worry, instead about your hopeless drinking sprees and chronic late -coming. Don't worry about my daughter! Don't call her a granny either! Maybe your girlfriends a re!

Girlfriends. Really? Is this not the same person who harps on the sacred obedience to relevancy in any given discussion? The other day I decided to put a stop to her wildness. I threatened Thola with a rough slap and before I could even lift my hand she was behaving the cry-baby way." I'll sue you for your abusive behavior". Her left index finger was pointing at my eyes threateningly. I was dismayed and disappointed when she quickly outlined them. What an array of them too. Let us count: Verbal Abuse. Sexual Abuse. Emotional Abuse. Economic Abuse. Use of Technology. Psychological Abuse.

She continued" I'll tell my parents that you're an abusive coward. Go ahead and hit me, my lawyers or the police will give you what you deserve. Not to mention the numerous

women's organizations. Have you heard of the women's slogan: Wathinta umfazi wathinta imbokodo?(You touch a woman, you touch a boulder). Don't dare press the wrong button. Abusers don't deserve to be in relationships, but belong to jails. You said what? You will slap me? Go on, do it. Try it and you'll rue the moment you slapped me! And the moment you were born. The law will give you a black eye in the twinkling of an eye".

She did not even excuse the pun, Good Heavens!

Mthwakaz'omuhle!(Good people!)That day she sobbed histrionically. I saw with my naked eyes a tornado of tears roll down her cheeks like I would drown in them. I did not touch her. No one can be sure! I was afraid partly because I was ignorant of a number of sections of the law on marriage, and partly because of the many newspaper stories of men who were either slapped with hefty fines or sent to long terms in prison for committing one domestic crime or another. It was real. Both male and female magistrates were merciless toward male offenders, so I concluded.

I decided to avoid possible controversies and confrontations by coming home early and spoiling her with a surprise gift or two. In spite of the stressful state of the economy we saw it fit for us to even cruise all the way to the Hwange National Park which is one of the ten largest wildlife heavens of Africa and the largest game reserve in the country. We were truly and absolutely thrilled by the sun-kissed grass that stretches for miles and miles and the awesome sight and number of the elephants at the waterhole. "Wow! No wonder this place is home to one of the world's largest populations of elephants!" she exclaimed, her happy hands touring "the Hwange" of my neck. Seeing the species of bird put us under a magic spell. Catching sight of Africa's majestic wildlife in the form of lions, giraffes, leopards, cheetahs, hyenas and wild dogs was pure delight. To cap a day of mystery and enchantment was the sight and the color of the sunset. It attracted and held our attention as if we were seeing the sun for the first time. It reminded us that we were on the blessed and naturally rich continent of Africa. Mother Africa. There is always something unique and magnetic about the African sun.

* * *

The following day we happily weaved our way to an impregnable marriage of grandeur and perfect beauty…in the name and form of the Victoria Falls!! For the umpteenth time, I fell in love with the Falls, and fell deeply and helplessly with my wife.

" Mosi-oa-Tunya! What a spectacular waterfall. Awe-inspiring sight. No wonder it's called The Smoke That Thunders", she crooned with an excitement of its own life. "No wonder it's one of the World's Seven Wonders! It's mystical. It's special. And I love you! I love you!" I chorused as I caressed her. She looked at me as if she would momentarily remind me of her gospel of relevancy before sensually whispering."Thank you. I love you too".

The beauty of love was in the air, in the driving seat again. I felt its beat thundering, burning and melting into my heart with a startling ferocity. It drew my heart to her heart and gave birth to a new fusion. In my dreams and thoughts, it murmured those rhythms of everlasting togetherness whose fire is fearless. I perched on its wings and wheels when I was far from her, and her nearness sang in full swing, in praise of a warmth that conquers the vagaries of her weather, her seasons and reasons. In her absence, I was haunted by a certain addictive hunger. I desired to be completed and healed by her closeness. There was an emptiness I could not bear or escape from. In my heart I banished the cyclicity with which our heated arguments occurred. Such contentions and shouts were consigned to the dustbin of past times. I was convinced that the road ahead had no blind turns or sharp humps.

When the way a man lives experiences changes, his friends are quick to pinpoint or pick it up, for good or bad reasons. A friend bumped into me one Friday afternoon at the nearest shop, and subjected me to what I termed silly grilling. "Why do you scarce yourself, SekaBuhle? Is everything fine?" "I was on vacation for two weeks. I'm doing fine, thanks". "What were you up to?"

"NakaBuhle and I visited the Hwange National Park and the mighty Victoria Falls?"

"Wow! The Falls! Do you know that it's largest waterfall in the world?"

"Of course. No wonder David Livingstone wrote: scenes so lovely must have been gazed upon by angels in their flight."

"But talking of Livingstone, don't you think you left out something about his claims?"

For a tempting moment, I looked at him without saying a word. Did he think I was a historian?

"Of course like Christopher Columbus, he claimed he discovered that breathtaking waterfall yet the Tonga and Makalolo people lived there. I think some historians have set that record right".

"OK, enough about those bloody claimants. When are you joining us for a drink or two?"

"My visit to Hwange and Victoria Falls was life-changing."

"I always say I don't care where you're, who you and what you do in this world, if you haven't been to the one and only

Victoria Falls then you haven't LIVED! Simple. That's my story. So what's your story?"

Turning on the ignition key of my car, I replied, "I quit drinking".

When I got home, my wife was cooking. I adored the idea!

The maid was playing with Buhle in our smallish backyard. I blamed my friend who had delayed me by asking little questions about trivia for the fact that my wife had arrived home earlier. I wanted to be the perfect gentleman of the house, the perfect husband of my lovely wife and the perfect father of my precious and precocious Buhle. As I relaxed on the couch, listening to some timeless musical ballads on the radio, I told myself: Muzi, now that you're on the right course, don't retreat or regret or listen to your friends anymore. Listen to the echoes and rhythms of your wife's wishes and desires. Let them be your command. Dance only to the beats of her heart. Don't delight in transitory and risky foolishness. Let it be in flight. In fright. For this is your sunlight. To this end, no more coming late, no more betting and drinking sprees with fooling friends, no more ...

I drifted into sleep. She woke me up after placing a huge multicolored plate on the circular table. In there was something finger-licking good. I could not resist salivating there and then. It was the magnetism, flavor and sight of isitshwala that had me coveting. This stiff maize meal is the staple food for many a Bulawayo resident. The maize corn is ground into flour called mealie-meal. With boiling water, the flour is cooked into thick porridge. For me, having isitshwala served with stewed vegetables and amasi for dinner was a feast made in heaven. Amasi is a Ndebele /Zulu/Xhosa term for fermented milk. In the olden days, amasi was traditionally prepared by preserving and storing unpasteurized cow's milk in a calabash container called igula. After fermentation, they would carefully separate umlaza, which is a watery substance from the creamy and tasty remainder, which is amasi.

"Please where is the clay pot and the wooden spoons?" I joked as we poured the thick liquid over the thick maize porridge

with great enthusiasm.

"I'm not culturally and ideologically bankrupt, but those are in the archives. That's where they belong now!", she thundered in a borrowed commander-in-chief-like voice.

"Where do I belong, my commander-in-in chief?" "You belong to me", she gestured a naughty gesture.

To say I was laughing like crazy is an understatement. I pitied my vibrating ribs.

I was fiercely proud of my turnaround, of my new behavior and of my renewed commitment to my family. To the best of my knowledge I was doing my level best to meet my family's needs. All that big change did not go unnoticed. My wife commended me for being there for them, for spending quality time with them. One day as I was driving home, I saw a road block ahead manned by two male traffic cops. They used internationally accepted hand signals to *beckon* and *stop me*. For a while I thought that their hand signals were professional and polite. However, it soon turned out that there was nothing honorable and courteous about their conduct. They just

wanted to solicit for a bribe.

"Look guys, my car's roadworthy and my papers are in order, so why should I grease your palms?"

"Have you just arrived in the country? Are you a novice?

Don't you know how bad the economy is?"

"I'm not immune from the economic hardships either."

"Then give us something, our throats are dry. We don't want to fine you".

"I don't have money. I'm busy. Please let me proceed?"

"You busy? We don't think so. Now keep us company."

They left me to my own devices. After waiting in vain for what seemed like an eternity, I thought about the boredom of explaining to my wife about the road ordeal and the possibility of an argument springing up, then I handed over a little bribe to one of the stubborn officers. Waiting was not worth the anxiety. In my fearful and imaginary world I could picture and hear my wife saying: You know they are corrupt to the core. Why couldn't you just stuff a five dollar note into an officer's mouth and drive away? That kind of money wouldn't make a huge difference. Maybe the road ordeal is just a mere excuse.

However, when I arrived home and narrated my road block story she exhibited amazing support, understanding and sympathy. Out of genuineness, frustration or an injured ego I vowed that no bribing police would ever get a penny from me in the future. I did not have hallucinations about the tragic reality on the ground. One did not need to be the brightest crayon in the box to know and acknowledge that corruption was in the DNA of the entire system of governance. I could not fathom how our once-beautiful nation had taken a turn for the worse. The rottenness of the system blew my socks off. Ordinary citizens were being ridiculed by the greedy and merciless authorities left, right and center.

* * *

After three months of abstinence from liquor, I could not stomach the craving for the brown bottle. I did not think of myself as having been a heavy drinker, neither did I consider my current condition as a potentially life-threatening one. The truth of the matter was that of late I was battling with bouts of mild anxiety and shakiness. I knew of a neighbor who tried to withdraw from drinking but ended up losing his wife and job because of serious complications like seizures and delirium tremens. I did not wish my situation to deteriorate to that level. No normal person would. Only a heartless person would wish such complications on one's worst enemy. I was no saint, but I just wanted to drown some of my miseries in beer and live a normal life. After all, in life we all seek to pursue happiness and abundance or even success in different ways. Every person has his or her life to live his or her own way and to employ his or her modus operand to deal with the complexities and infirmities of life in the best manner he or she sees fit.

I felt like I was leading a dry lie, living a double life. Maybe I was not even living. I was merely existing. Life could not be restricted just to moving from point A to point B, then back and forth. From home to work, then work back home. What a routine! Was I a marionette? Was I a robot? Was I being remote-controlled from a certain point? I missed my friends, their crazy jokes, music and chats. I yearned for their company. I wanted to live again. It was in my interest to take back myself. I sought to kick out the hypocrite in me. I desired to discover myself. I wanted to be me again. That Friday I hooked up with my friends at Mpompi's Cocktail and we had six sizzling hours of catching up. Throwing caution out of the "first window" was not on the cards that day. Therefore, I took a few sips of my favorite beer as we chatted and joked. Then I departed for home, promising to catch up with them the following Friday at the same time and venue.

In spite of my lateness that day my wife did not become a drama queen, a person I was somehow apprehensive of. She did not bring up the issue of my lateness in our discussion. In fact, I told her she was the loving queen of my heart. I did not see it coming, but she had something up her sleeve.

"Muzi, next time the king and the queen have a vacation, let them make the best of it...Again! The visits to Hwange and Victoria Falls left an unforgettable and indelible taste in my mouth".

"Indeed, I share the same sentiment. As we say, it trickles down into the same windpipe!"

"My word, some of your direct translations knock the hell out of my sanity! They translate...or rather transform me into a proud

African queen! Anyway, I was thinking...what about trickling all the way to an archipelago of ....wait for this...one hundred and fifteen islands in the Indian Ocean off East Africa? Wouldn't that be one of the most wonderful and romantic destinations we've ever embarked on as a couple?"

I know I was a bit tipsy but if her question did not get me sobering up, it got me thinking about possible ways of eluding the gist of the discussion.

"Ahh...ahh you mean...?"At that point in time I just wanted to find a hole and disappear into or to be chocked by an invisible but stubborn bone or to decry being a victim of a mouth-gagging spell, and mumble being struck by a sudden speech impediment. Those are times when I wished I were a facile actor or a slippery orator. The one who slips through fingers and fences when everybody else thinks they have him completely cornered.

"I mean the Seychelles of course! Are you okay, darling?"

"I'm. Yes. I'm. It's... just that the way you describe this place...it's mouth-watering. It's irresistible. The way you introduce the idea of traveling to the Seychelles. Yes ".

I witnessed her face beam and beam with pride and happiness. I wanted to tell her that my "Yes" did not in any way mean I was in agreement with her Seychelles suggestion. No! But I could not say "NO" either. Talk of a scenario where one's response is taken out of context. My Goodness! For me, it was a futile verbal battle. She was winning that game hands down because she was consolidating her victory by saying:

"My king, thank you so much. You've made my day. It doesn't require a visa to go to that island. We won't have to spend a fortune on their five star hotels, I know.

I picture us visiting the exciting beach of *Port Launay*, the Valle de Mai plantation in Praslin and the Anse Source D'Argent in La Digue, and then witnessing an unforgettable sunset! God willing, we could end up going to the Mauritius,

another bastion of fun for romantic tourists."

Thulani is my friend in the true sense of the word. Yes, the one and only Thulani whose name literally means "Shut Up"—qualifies to be called my chum. The other chaps I hang out with at Ziyanetha's Bar or Mpompi's Cocktail or at any other watering hole in the city are mere acquaintances, but because beer drinking tends to foster a spirit of togetherness and happiness among the drinkers, I call them friends. It is in that spirit of sharing, I find myself loosely refereeing to "my cabinet at the counter" as my friends or better still, brothers and sisters. The tricky part of the reference, though, is that some other brothers and sisters end up "hitting it out" big time. "Shut Up" who, contrary to the essence and meaning of his name, hardly shuts up about anything in general and those romantic relationships or one night stands in particular. He describes them as "incestuous in opposite".

* * *

Soon it was Friday, and after work I drove straight to Mpompi's Cocktail. I had been taking sips of my favorite "food" on a daily basis that week, and so on that Friday evening I made a conscious decision to take camel-like gulps of beer, as if to make up for lost time. Actually, it was going to be serious business. Somewhere at the back of my mind, it was billed THE HOMECOMING OF THE WISE WATERS. After all, the daily sips had effectively cured me of anxiety and shakiness. I wanted to celebrate. I wanted to kiss beer passionately. I wanted to teach beer a lesson it would not forget for a long, long time. That I could swallow up an ocean of it and still drive home to my family like all responsible fathers and husbands. I scooped mouthfuls as I sought to quench my thirst. When my friend Thulani showed up, the first thing he said was:" Muzi, shut up! Already you're mumbling and talking to yourself. Really? Shame! Remember, you're learning to run afresh, so take it easy. Beer's older than your great grandfather. Don't let it drink you up!" He quickly disappeared. When he came back he gritted his teeth, "What I saw in the gentlemen's bathroom

was not gentle at all but disgusting. I know, it's a public loo. All these men here who appear to be clean and normal must be fooling our eyes.

Show me a clean man, and I'll show you a clean toilet, too. I hereby propose a new designation for the effective management and protection of these public amenities—the position of TSI, an honorable acronym for Toilet Shit Inspector. It's not one of the easiest, sweetest and healthiest management jobs to do on this planet. What with careless and messy facility users coming in for relief ,making of sorts of not-so-nice music, going out, and in the process stretching one's patience thin but it's a position in which one would have the enviable authority and privilege to say: Dear TU for Toilet User, let's see what legacy you're leaving behind here. Oh no, not so fast, go back! I wish it were fun but it's foul. That this is your big foul mess is not a subject for debate. Now do yourself a big favor. Clean up or pay up. Never mind the size of the shit, the shit-wiping penalty is currently pegged at $20:00. Let me tell you what we don't take. We don't take shit from anyone here, you included!"

I was battling and shaking with uncontrollable laughter as

Thulani spoke at length about what he thought about some toilet users. Perhaps there are two major things I have noticed about Thulani. The first one is his sense of humor. I have always advised him to take up stand-up comedy as a profession but he has not heeded my advice to this day. The second observation is that I believe he is always drunk or mad in his special way. He is drunk before even taking the slightest sips of alcohol. He does not need to be certified by a medical doctor that he is crazy. I think it is his peculiar craziness and drunkenness that has endeared him to me and a lot of people, especially ladies. Man, damn, is he not a piece of mess that can bring down the roof of an auditorium?

I will not talk about other "cabinet members" who, besides exchanging greetings and goodbyes, said very little about themselves and everything else.

There is a certain air of muteness that speaks a library of possibilities. I could see that even my vocal friend Thulani handled them with a bit of care, if not trepidation.

I and Thulani were the cabinet members present that day. That day, together we swam in beer until my judgment of everything I saw or thought or felt was one flighty, amusing and rollerskating experience. I kept on throwing bottles at Thulani, and he would not disappoint. He would reciprocate in style. I knew I could put trust in him on that front. And those were not empty bottles. They were filled with ice-cold beer. They filled us with joy of joys. What happened next, I was told...

It was around 11:00 in the morning on Saturday when my wife woke me up for breakfast. I was dizzy and weak. My head was telling me: now is the time for the hangover to dance its dance. Yesterday, you were delirious and fantastic. Today, you're the delicious food for the hangover. I yawned and staggered my way to the bathroom. When I was at the kitchen table, reluctantly sipping the renowned and loved *Mazoe Orange* Crush *my wife broke the news.*

"Last night your friend Thulani and a certain noisy female drunkard brought you home. At first I thought maybe you had been involved in an accident or you had been mugged. You were sloshed. I mean bombed! Plastered. Yes, your clothes were plastered with vomit! Check them in the washing basket to get some incontrovertible evidence. You were leaning on them, and making some annoying and mental circuiting noise with your feet. That lady's raucous voice probably woke up Buhle. It gave me some high blood pressure. If beer made my voice loud and unpleasant to listen to, or woke up innocent children, I would quit it. Muzi, you were leaning on that bitch,

with her left hand around your waist. Really? If I were you, I would give up drinking. In life, I've learned that if something brings about disgrace, bravely kick it out of your life, no matter how beautiful or nice it is".

One of our former "cabinet members" once said," In life we do silly things and revel or later regret. That's normal and acceptable. Life is a race to outpace our weaknesses and challenges. To outgrow our foolishness. To be better citizens we must have the zeal and zest to go beyond our foolishness and prudence." I wondered what he meant, what had come over him to be that preachy. Whilst I was wondering he quit beer and started leading a different life. That was his choice, his decision, his life. I could not kick Thulani out of my life. I could not kick beer out of my life. Not now. I could not see life beyond our cabinet. Not in the foreseeable future. All that meant something. It meant the recurrence of yelling, arguments and counter-arguments at home. It was not long before NakaBuhle started saying I was good at kissing the mouths of a variety of beer mugs or other women. She claimed she was sleeping fitfully because l was not giving her enough attention and affection. I told her to shut up because her cries were not my lullaby. She cried more loudly! I am sure our neighbors' eyebrows were easily raised. That they are always on the lookout and are showing too much curiosity about other people's affairs is written all over their ears, lips, eyes, faces and actions. It is alarming and amazing that even their sons and daughters are cutting their teeth in the business of eavesdropping and gossiping as if it is a lucrative venture.

NakaBuhle is an executive secretary. Courtesy of my encouragement and support she has reached this level, professionally. I am happy for her. I am proud of her academic and professional achievements. Let me go back in time... You see, her father paid her school fees up to grade seven and that was as far as my father-in law deemed fit. At that stage, my wouldbe father -in -law must have folded his arms with contentment, and said: you have the wings, fly away and conquer the world.

I think she flew towards my direction, and with my sharp catapult of heart, l aimed at her, and scooped my target with charm. Bingo! The rest is history. The big day arrived in style. At our wedding people danced till toes literally peeped through shoes. That day her mouth crackled with love, wit and humor. We were cozy. She was besotted with love. I was a river overflowing with love. There was the lovey-dove spirit that kept our hearts, jumping, pumping, jumping, pumping in that order for several days on end. The love bug was upon us. When people are bitten by the love bug, they breastfeed on their milk with an astonishing excitement. Sometimes, they become children without even noticing it. Love is endowed with impressive transforming qualities.

Then, the following day, there we were on honeymoon in a hilly lodge. I must have been drunk with her love, because l fell off a little rock we had seated on, rolled over downward three times. Hurriedly, my heroine pulled me up and sat her knight in armor on her laps. l was seeing several confusing stars of dizziness. I exclaimed with a tinge of embarrassment: Honey, what a free-falling honeymoon. Who said miracles don't happen?

My suit was in a mess. She asked me how I felt, before uttering countless "sorrys" and, brushing my suit with her tender hands as if it were cobwebs. I said: my nurse of tenderness and politeness, I am perfectly fine. How can I be disturbed and distracted by this trivial thing when your angelic light shines on me? This was in spite of the fact that I had just escaped the fall with one little bruise on my forehead.

* * *

A few months after the wedding I could see the sparkle of happiness in my parents' eyes when they saw her. They were aglow with joviality. They affectionately and respectfully called her malukazana (bride). She respected them in a way that made me a proud connoisseur of decorum and diligence. She worked like a burrowing mole day in day out, making our homestead one of the most beautiful homes to live in. She never burrowed into the blankets like when the rays of the sun peeped into her room and announced morning time.

These days when she is off-duty she is sleepy and lazy all day long. Alas, as if that were not enough headache for me for a single day, she accuses my mother of witchcraft. She also blames the woman who brought me into this world for many unfounded things like gossiping and malevolence and competing with her as if she is my wife too! I AM SPEECHLESS! She maligns my mother and expects me to side with her! Even with shovels and shovels of zwanamina being subtly offloaded into my mouth, I won't do such a crime of blind partisanship!

Is this her way of thanking my dear mother for bringing her an accountant husband like me? I have not accused her mum of witchcraft. No. Of course, my father-in-law has, on several occasions! He even said prophets have confirmed it. I have refused to rope myself in that issue.

However, what I know is that she has on many occasions implored my wife to respect me and avoid labeling me a hopeless drunkard.

I recall the good old days. My wife was very understanding and respectful then. She always knelt down while serving me

with food. She referred to me as baba. Not hopeless drunkard, I dare say! She was at my beck and call, as they say, doing laundry and keeping the house clean. At that time we did not have a domestic worker. She never said bad things about my friend, Thulani. No.

I felt like a real man. I was proud of her as my wife. I treasured the respect she had for me. She never called it fear. No single day ever passed by with her arguing with me over trivial things. I do not remember her quarreling with me, calling me an ever-bossy and righteous husband. Or telling me to modernize my ways and thinking.

Nowadays we argue about almost everything. From parenting ways, to what TV programs to watch, to why I do not take her out for an expensive lunch downtown or why I cannot or do not call her every day. As it is she says I promised to take her on a pleasure trip to the Seychelles and Mauritius but she is still waiting in vain like Bob Marley. When I tell her that we do not have sufficient money to undertake such trips, she accuses me of reneging on my words. When I tell her she misunderstood me or is misquoting me, she hits out at me, saying I am behaving like political vultures of the land who forever bemoan the effects of bad journalism when their dishonesty is exposed.

My wife claims that she is worried. She says I have become a nomadic and aimless night rider. Is this not an insult, really? Does going out with friends for a good drink amount to drifting? She also accuses me of not being fashion-conscious. I have not accused her of being a spendthrift, and one of these days I shall say it in a loud and clear way!

Oh, how can I bring back those days? During those good days, she did not spend money on useless things. Maybe, she does so to send a statement that it is her money, after all. She never complained when I came home late. I did it every day. There was no issue. I did not need to attend her boring kangaroo court sections after that. She never bothered to ask me where l was, and what the heck l was up to.

Now... It is a crime. A serious crime for that matter. It's like l have committed some unpardonable murder or what. I don't get it. How on earth can coming late at home be equated with committing a gruesome murder?

Oh, l wish l could turn back the hand of time. I mean going back to those great days when she treated me like a king. She showered rivers and rivers of love upon me. I bathed in her love. I drowned in her love. I swam to safety in her love. l cherished the respect she had for me, and the care and love she poured out. The humility with which she received me from work. Her beaming face was my favorite sight. A kiss was never an issue. She never questioned why I sent her to stay a few months in my rural home with my parents. She obliged and worked in the fields and fetched firewood and water like all good wives. Now she sees too much. Eh... In my mother she sees a witch! In her absence she sees mistresses and unofficial co-wives. She says l smile too often with our helpmate. Am l supposed to frown at her because she is our domestic worker? Is she not human? Is she a plague? Is that the reason why my wife is firing domestic workers like a mother changing a child's nappies?

She won't visit my rustic parents. Of kisses she ransoms me to them in the mornings and afternoons with a hungry seriousness that can huddle me to the Hague for crimes against humanity! Abdication of the kissing game is no option. I did not know that kisses can be timed or fixed. Like...what time is it now? It's 6 O'clock on the dot. It's kisses time, people!

Thulani once warned me... He said I was buying myself an axe that would be used on me by helping her further her studies. Right he was ... Dead right. She is recalcitrant and arrogant. She forgets I paid through the nose for her. I ask her to make me some tea after work and what does she say? She says I forget that she was at work too! Is that a polite way of responding to one's husband, really? I know parents taught her good manners. She has been misled by her so-called friends and human rightists. The tragedy of it is that she cannot see the damage that is being caused by those over-zealous nosepokers. To make matters worse, she is blind to her failings and follies.

Sometimes she uses big words to insult me. For example, she has the temerity to say I am a lazy egotist who after work comes home and rots in the sofa with crossed legs while reading the paper till amen and amen! What cheek is this? She has the audacity to remind me of the presence and responsibilities of our domestic worker! Can you imagine what she says? She declares: if you want loyalty please buy a dog! I am your wife, not your servant or slave? This is not a master/servant relationship. Please stop living in the past. How can a woman and a wife for that matter say that to her man? I am not supposed to be her king? Am I not one? Am I abusing her by asking that she makes me tea me, just once in a week, for I am not a big fan of that beverage?

My friend makes me laugh at times. For example, he boasts of having divorced three times in his life. Of the first divorce, he says he caught his first wife red-handed, wearing a pair of new blue jeans when he came back home unceremoniously one day. I question him: what was the crime, Thulani? Did you suspect that some man had bought her the trousers? He says that is not the point. The fact of the matter is that he did not allow his wife and girlfriends to wear trousers! He says he has since had change of heart over the trousers issue. "Amen, that's the way to go, man!" I enthuse. To myself I am asking: wait a minute, did I hear what he has just said? If NakaBuhle thinks I'm a complete die hard, would she not say without mincing her words that he's a lost dinosaur without some loincloth or animal skin on? I bet my last dollar she would not describe him as a cultural conservative. After all, she has, on my occasions, told me that she has very little respect for him because he is an irredeemable fossil. I have not told her what I think of her friends too. One thing is certain: they discuss me in bad light.

Thulani tells me that his second wife was "fired" for secretly keeping an ominously looking plastic vibrator under their bed. I am not sure whether it was making noise, vibrating crazily from underneath in his presence or committed other crimes in his absence. The third wife was shown the red card after seeking to serve him with food spiced with "taste me". I ask him how did he know that there was korobela (a man-stupefying herb) in the food? He denies being a superstitious man. He claims to have had a dream the previous night that warned him not to eat food from his wife for a week. So he says on that stupid day, he just asked the wife to tuck into her food because he did not have an appetite. She also said she did not have an appetite. That was too much of a coincidence, he says.

My friend tells me that a woman who wears a garment with an image of another man or even another woman is not to be trusted. She is too dangerous to live with. He says the picture displaced on a lady's T-shirt should be that of her husband or boyfriend, period. I say to him: Friend, wait a minute. Are you not being unrealistic about the loyalty you expect from women? Please don't take umbrage at what l am about to say… Does this not border on plain naivety and male pig chauvinism?

He says no, he is being practical and prudent. In his words: Women are hearers and perceptive people and as such they tend to be influenced easily by what they hear or see on a daily basis. They can see how one walks, l mean her gait, how and what one eats, how one woman's make-up has been over-applied, how her colors clash in a clearly vicious way, how she over-dresses when she goes to church, and so forth and so forth. Petty jealousies and over-analysis of trivia are things that are not a stranger to the world of women. Men may not see all these things or even bother a whit about them. Now here comes the problem. Women may hear something at first and feel an outburst of disgust rioting inside their bodies.

That is good. However, after some time, when a person keeps on bombarding them with the same message, they tend to give in. With a mocking chuckle he adds, "The hypodermic needle theory implied mass media had a direct, immediate and powerful effect on its audiences. It just stopped short of hitting the snake on the head and concluding: especially female audiences! How often do you propose to a woman and she says she is not interested in oneself at all, yes, no, no , not at all, forget it in one's lifetime. Then eventually after 'shooting' or 'injecting' her with appropriate messages designed to trigger a desired response: boom, she makes a big U-turn and says Yes! Yes! Yes! You're welcome!"

Then he tells me of charismatic churches in the city that have installed Point of Sale (POP) machines at their premises to afford the congregants an opportunity to pay their tithes and offerings using plastic money as a means of countering cash shortages. I applaud it. He chuckles."Hmm. You're saying amen to that. OK. What can I say? Have you seen how some of the modern crooks and impostors waylay women in church? They say they are not of flesh, but look at how selfish they are!

They tell the good women to go to some bushy or secluded place for special prayers, and the good sheep go, only for the shepherd to eat them up. Women. The wolves in sheep skin tell them the holy spirit seeks to get into your bodies unhindered by dresses and all, so next Sunday, please ladies, be nudists, and they shout: Amen! Amen, pastor! Amen! Some are asked to buy special tickets to paradise, and who are they to say no? Others are ordered to feast on leaves like cows and gulp fuels like vehicles and they sheepishly play along. What gullibility is this? Church chicanery has never been more fashionable". I tell him to put the blame on bogus male pastors who are taking advantage of the ignorance, desperation and vulnerability of their congregants to further their selfish ends.

* * *

One cold Friday night in the month of June we were at

Mpompi's Cocktail when he continued with his tirade about women. I said to him: Friend, l think you make women look really cheap, childish and gullible. Not only that. You are also saying they cannot be trusted, and this raises issues about your possible personal indiscretions of insecurity. Don't you feel insecure and inadequate? He responded with a somehow arrogant cut –the- crap -woman-ruled marionette chuckle." Not, not at all. If you miss one taxi, and another one heaves in sight, you flag it down, it pulls over and you hop into it. I am secure because l have enough ammunition to deal with any eventuality".

He took a long gulp before asking rhetorically," Do you see Methuseli at our cabinet meetings these days? No, he has no one else to blame for his stupidity, emasculation and incarceration."

"What do you mean by emasculation and incarceration? Is he in jail?" I inquired.

"Here's the thing. I think his unrestrained wife has put him under house arrest. I'm talking of real issues when I say women have to be guided, advised or restricted in one way or the other if our societies are to be respectful, peaceful and stable again.

Technology comes at a cost.

He told me that his wife was live on Facebook telling the world that her husband was spending money on beer and possibly on side chicks, and asking people to help her deal with her situation.

What kind of nonsense is this? Where are we going as a people, as a society, as men and women?

I didn't skirt around the issue. I said to him: I believe you've two major things at play to address here. I don't care whether it's a 4 Chan, AirBNB, Facebook, Flickr, Skype, Google+,Instagram, LinkedIn, MySpace, Periscope, Pinterest, Reddit, Snapchat account, there has to be some consensus on either you monitor such a social media account or it is put to rest by being invalidated once and for all".

"What was Methuseli's response to your suggestion?", I probed with interest.

"He said he was outraged, not by his wife's Facebook drama, but by my disregard for invasion of privacy and my level of foolishness! Really? He added that I should just shut up like the message and meaning behind my name. I said: OK. Let's

wait and see who'll have the last laugh."

The moment l slapped my eyes on her, l saw somebody l thought was worth marrying. Someone to treat as one's queen for the rest of my life. I wanted to give her the opportunities that her family could not offer her. I did not know that l was giving her wings to fly away, and defy some of my instructions as her husband. I thought I was parachuting her out of darkness into the light. Now she uses that light to dazzle me. Can you imagine that gratitude! She is elusive and slippery l don't know how to deal with her wildness. I don't know how to make her see that all l want is to be treated like a king.

The other day l asked, "Please treat me like your king. Am I not your king?" She said," First treat me like your queen, then l'II crown you my king. If you treat me like a little rag, l will treat you like crap as well! That's the modern matrix of marriage. It's a give- and -take equation."

I don't get it. I think the institution of marriage is more sacred than her warped equation, or whatever it is. I give her concrete examples that her equality dream is nothing but a mere dream or a pie in the sky. For example, women athletes don't compete on the same tracks with their male counterparts. It is the same story when it comes to wrestling. Why? And, of course they make more noise than they exhibit their wrestling dexterity on the ring. l go on and on... "Some universities demand lower minimum academic entry points for women than men. Why?"

She counters like one boxer who gets a blow on the cheek and in turn unleashes her knock back on her opponent with a hungry vengeance. She claims I make a series of incredulous claims. I over-analyze. I over-simplify. In short, l drivel fulltime! I babble big time! I must grow up. She claims that she is too snowed under to listen to some of my gibberish.

Too what? And what has snow got to do with this? I live in Africa, l know little about snow! l have often warned her against using idioms that are not local or relevant. The same person who complains now and then that l don't phone her as frequently as she would like me to, is what? Is too snowed under-whatever the hell it means-to listen to me! This is weirder than the word weird itself. It makes no sense at all. She opens her mouth and says what? I drivel! Mthwakazi (People)! I drivel full-time? I am an overgrown baby? Is this not a big insult. Again.

Again. I am not surprised that our male elders kept a little rod or a knobkerrie. Thulani, too says he keeps a knobkerrie in their bedroom.

I remember Thulani telling me one day: They harp on rights, rights and rights. What's right about this insolence? I'm not going to pander to the politicians' whims and tricks. Politicians are a breed of opportunists. They're always looking for votes. Votes are about numbers. If these insects called equal rights are like this, then l don't want them in my home. Let the politicians who give these women these so called rights keep them! Here... Nope! No, please, Mr Politician, in my backyard, don't off load your so-called rights. My cultural lights are bright enough to keep us going in the right direction as a family. Tell you what, in my house l am supposed to be the king. Fullstop. Rule your country and l rule my household. Right? That politician who gives women these rights must be told, he has gone too far in his search for elusive votes.

If politicians are not stopped dead in their tracks, next time, they would possibly be telling us how to love our

wives in accordance with the provisions of the constitution. They could enshrine in that document things like: how to caress or kiss them or how to care for them when they are pregnant or moody or on periods and all. Our customs or norms will be relegated to nothing. Yet our traditions are clear on these things. These crazy laws will invade our privacy. I won't be shocked if one day or one year some of the overenthusiastic legislators pass skewed laws that would proclaim the superiority of the womenfolk over the menfolk. Laws on how to do women's bidding in any given situation at any given time, how to make them happy, free, complete and proud. Now every day we hear ear-deafening noises about uplifting them and making them company executives, national leaders, church leaders, and so on and so forth. Men, open your minds and eyes, these silly laws on how to live in perpetual bondage for the sake and love of these descendants of Eve are just one step toward such an unfortunate scenario. Our emasculation. We're done for if we don't act now. Every day

we hear of court rulings that are in their favor.

Like a duck taking to water, my friend, sometimes talks in parables like a pastor taking to the pulpit. He claims Eve, the women's progenitor yielded to the serpent's deception and ended up eating fruit from the forbidden tree. What else did she do? She gave some of the fruit to Adam. What a temptress! Wasn't Adam told that he could till the ground and eat freely of all the trees in the garden, except for a tree of the knowledge of good and evil? Eve, created from one of Adam's ribs caused the fall of man. There they stood in the glare of nudity. Was this Eve's sense of fashion? These lawyers, like the biblical snakehave yielded to the women's tempting tricks and demands.

That's it. We are trapped! That's why marriage is no longer sacred, and societal disintegration and debauchery is on the increase. Governments, families, judges and lawyers are trapped in a futile cycle of trying to meet all the women's endless demands for this and that. This is crazy and sad. When are they going to wake up and also look into men's rights and plight? If we give in to all the women's rights for this and that, then where is our male pride, where is our kingly manhood, where is our outstanding manliness? And this world would be upside-down. We cease to be real men. Men...because we are tucked into trousers? What a shrill cry. Women wear trousers these days and, in a big way, too. Maybe my friend should breathe into life a social movement against women? Otherwise what use is this rant?

My friend says some befuddled men are even claiming that women are better leaders. "What crap! They say if all national leaders and presidents were female this world would be much more peaceful, orderly and nicer to live in. These are, of course, myopic males or blind worshipers of women who have been fed too much man-stupefying herbs," He claims that each time he tells them that their dreams are a Utopia because women are always at loggerheads with one another, and this stands to reason that such countries would not be in speaking terms with other nations— they tell him that he should stop making wild, wild claims in his warped way, in his foolish head. He tells me that in spite of telling the "worshipers" of women that nations led by women would suffer in terms of bilateral relations, he says they continue calling him names.

He goes on to say besides, in reality, women are too emotionally-charged creatures who always fall victim to petty jealousies, and such disposition cannot augur well for peace! No bilateral relations, trade suffers, the economies suffer, and the peoples of the world suffer. He claims no matter how much sense he tries to ingrain into the heads of "the worshipers of women" they fire back at him, accusing him of being a brazen, brutal anachronistic misogynist, whatever those big words mean. He reveals that during one of those heated debates other men asked him whether he really hated his mother, auntie, sister and grandmother so much that he

would celebrate if these were abused on a daily basis by men. He says that day he was at pains to explain his stance. He confesses that such a question caught him with his pants down. He had egg on his face. However, he had to conjure up something. Then he claims that the next thing he found himself yelling at them:" My mother is my mother! My sister is my sister! My auntie is my auntie! My grandmother is my grandmother! Stop comparing them to my wife or girlfriend. Call me anything, use all the demeaning words you can think of, one day a woman, and possibly your wife or girlfriend will divulge your darkest secret, and only then will you know better than to take down another man".

Though he might be a bit fanatical about this issue, I think my friend is right about some of these rights that women are clamoring for. Let the lawyers go on promulgating laws in favor of women and see who will have the last laugh. Rights plus women equals wildness. These sympathizers will reap what they have sown. For the so call-equal rights drive the womenfolk crazy and wild! I have never seen a single sane woman who listens to what politicians say!

* * *

I plough my hands onto "the thighs" of the brown bottle. I caress them. For a while I admire the structure and contents of the container as if it holds the center of my very existence. Gleefully I mumble to myself: I'm having a ball. Beer, l can't bid you farewell. If there has to be divorce in my life, then it should not affect you. No woman can stand in between you and me. The world would be dead hell without you! Dead and dull. Women of all colors, sizes and shapes- though they light up the world in one way or the other- would not mean a thing if you are nowhere! Zilch! Transcendent waters you swim me in bliss and triumph! Wise waters you transport me to the most amazing zones filled with fun and friends. You're better than rollerskating. You're long-lasting.

My chubby mouth proudly digs deep into the bubbly depths of the cocktail waters. Not once, neither twice, but thrice. And this is thoroughly and religiously executed in style by any definition or standard. The mouthfuls seem to rejuvenate me into a reverie of acrobatic jiving and diving like my bones are truly elastic. One lady on a mission does a calculated get-down with me -like we share a placental affinity which cannot be broken- while pampering me with flirtatious winks and strong body whiffs and whispers. I am elated.

But... a hand suddenly tows me from the back. I scream: Whose bloody hands are these? Is it a bloody sin or crime to enjoy one's bloody money in this bloody country? Son of... But I quickly discover who the party-popper is.

It's Thulani. His bulging stomach is obscured by the crimson double breasted suit that he is flaunting today.

"Nice suit, my man", I observe.

I fidget rather clumsily on the cozy chair like any time from now I would be heading for the restroom. Thulani extends his "sincere" apologies. "Even nicer is this queen who's keeping me company. I'm sincerely sorry to say I had to wrench you off that female with stunning looks. You were certainly socking it out with a woman who can curse every innocent child in the world with a series of nightmares after slapping their innocent eyes on her!"

I know that Thulani's talks on women are usually filled with pride. I remember Thulani saying: Women's wings have to be clipped. Don't let her be an opposition to your position. The problem is that you behave like a little playground and walkover for your wife. Have a ball in your yard, be the undisputed king of the house. No woman under this sun can play antics on me. Forget. Not even my wife touches me if l don't want. I can swing up into the air and sting her like a disturbed bee. Do you know what happens if you touch a lively mopani worm? It vomits out on you! I'm untouchable. I'm a lively mopani worm. I'm a grenade. My wife does my bidding. She can't cow me into submission. No ways. She knows her place. I can't be messed around with.

"SekaBuhle, it is my singular honor and privilege to proclaim: meet the queen who treats me with brimming care, one whose favor and affection I won ... and one I love like no other in a

world teeming with rough and rogue partners!"

I take a gaze at my friend's latest conquest and utter,

"Hi Queen of his eyes". Our hands clasp together and boy oh boy, I feel the amazing crudeness of her hands. I am almost tempted to ask: How many houses have you plastered so far?

I look at the bums...then the face, next, down to the legs. My eyes take a flying tour of the stomach, the legs, the face and the bums again. Lord, beauty is in the eye of the beholder... Thulani was not frog-marched into this! If l were in a toilet l would be spitting out some saliva in celebration of a friend's great find! Yeah. One man's girlfriend is another man's...I don't know. I think she is from another planet. Probably one of the most recently discovered ones. The elders were right to say a good knobkerrie is the one you chop off a tree in far and foreign lands. She smiles with the mischief and pride of an innocent school girl who has just been told by her flattering and fooling boyfriend that she is the best thing to have ever happened to him since he landed on Mother Earth!

"Hi. Miss Thenjiwe Hlahla is the name to watch. And she will bring you a lady almost beautiful as the one you're fixing or rather feasting your eyes on. Yeah. Stay close to this beauty for more!",so brags the mini-skirted slim lady with a wink and a smile, resting her equally tiny if not somehow lifeless right hand on the left expansive shoulder of her lover.

With the greetings and introductions done, we get down to business. The cabinet meeting is in session. We down the bottles with an appetite that can surely rival that of three thirsty camels in a desert. But if I were to give away a "camel's trophy" to one of the threesome, beyond a shadow of a doubt -Thulani's new release would easily be the medalist. She beats both of us at our game. There is something I am not comfortable with. Fancy somebody taking gulps with a determination that defies description. She is baptizing herself with the wise waters like a convert who seeks to wash away her most stubborn imperfections on Earth.

Meanwhile Thulani is running out of adjectives to describe Thenjiwe."She's unique, mature, talented and intelligent. Not to mention how exciting it is to hang out with her. Our first date was out of this world. I'll never forget it. There's nothing like that experience". I am wondering: so Thulani has just had his best date ever? Wonders would never cease for sure. It would be interesting to hear what his wife could make out of this confession, if she were to get wind of it.

He goes on showering praises on her. "I go with the eagles because these birds have great vision that allows them to detect prey during flight. Talk of powerful talons and beaks. Their good eyesight helps them find food, whilst their strong feet help them hold that food, and their curved beaks are effective for tearing flesh. Eagles have legs and feet feathered to the toes. They build big stick nests. What do I mean by all this? Let me put things in context. Thenji is short for Thenjiwe. My lovely Thenji, may look small, with her tiny legs and all, but she has strong personality. She's the epitome of intelligence and physical stamina. I also call her my wild horse because she can gallop with amazing grace. She can sense danger from a distance. So today, you don't have to worry and look over your shoulders. She's the one who suggested this venue. With her we soar without being seen or caught by party-spoilers.

Trust me. Whenever I'm with her I feel like I've been nestled on the climax of joys".

I nod with my head. The nagging thing is her belching and frothing mouth! Sorry times ten but all this behavior puts me off! To myself I am protesting: All this makes beerdrinking feel like a pain rather than a pleasure. Beer-drinking is pure sweetness itself. This over-excited fellow spoils it with her sourness. Honestly, this is not funny at all.

This bloody unimpressive plasterer gives beer-drinking a bad name. Her hands! Lord of Lords! They almost lacerated my fingers! At her back or on her hands words like: You shake hands with me at your own peril should be inscribed boldly and clearly. She reminds me of a jagged water lizard called Uxamu! (A monitor lizard). Not a soaring eagle. No! I beg to differ.

Thenjiwe seems to be supercharged with love. Now and then her hot kisses land on Thulani's neck, lips, cheeks and forehead with an amazing hunger. She even pinches her lover's back with a giggle or two. Maybe she's a flesh-eating eagle, after all. She has spotted her food. Is this her first time to fall in love? Seems the love bug has bitten her for the first time? No, this passion, or rather infatuation is not right. She needs to slow down. She must be slapped with a ticket for over-speeding!

Honestly, I am not amused at all. Her giggling does not make things any better either. The three of us find ourselves discussing politics, wondering whether it is imperative that we vote in the light of what has been happening over a period of more than thirty-six years. Polls after polls have been nothing but a cycle of mysterious fiascoes. What with the so-called ruling party with its deep-rooted meanness giving every normal soul or citizen a series of nightmares.

"Guys, I'm tired of voting for ghosts", I declare.

"What exactly do you mean by ghosts?" Thulani asks.

I explain, "Voting has always been a gimmick, a rat race. It's a waste of time. We're being taken for a ride during election time." Thenjiwe coughs in a rather heavy, guttural way before uttering, "Gents, those fraudsters will be enmeshed in their mess. The world will know too much about their chicanery to shore them up. Facing international isolation, I don't see them performing miracles that will take the country forward. Remember they are experts in running down the country. They are shameless and unwavering. They always rig and boast. However, they will never 'rig the economy'. That's where the taste of the pudding is in. Dogs during copulation get really so stuck together that their movement becomes a sad, static circus."

I nod and nod with my head as if saying: for the first time, you're talking. For the first time, you're saying something sensible and pertinent. I add, "The problem is that they have no conscience whatever. They find pleasure in inflicting pain or injury. Consider the damage they have done to our past, our history and heritage. Our economy's in tatters. Think of the horrifying abductions, disappearances, killings, persecutions, agonies and indignities they have visited upon the poor citizens, the opposition, the innocent activists and protesters over the past thirty-six years. Do you, for a moment, think they are remorseful? Don't you see that if they had any modicum of humanity they would have either repented and resigned or stopped pursuing populist policies and programs? They are just shameless, malicious, soulless, holier-than thou beasts, charlatans and rogues who'll continue looking for scapegoats, near and far, lying and looting, suppressing forces of justice, singing praises to the past ad infinitum whilst the ordinary people in the meantime sink deeper and deeper into

social-economic misery. It's such a pity, really."

Suddenly Thenjiwe changes the subject and turns to me.

"How's your wife? I hear she's giving you a tough time. She runs the show.'"

I pause for a while processing her question and looking at Thulani who in turn looks away.

"She's fine, thanks for asking".

My goodness! That's taboo! Who the heck does she think she's to say I'm being given a tough time? Is she the United Nations Chief? While admittedly I could be having differences and disagreements with my wife, that alone does not give this complete stranger a license to play a weird peacemaker or poke her little nose into my marriage. She runs the show. So what? That's none of her business. If she's an eagle then she should know where to soar to. Fly away from my marriage. Mind your business.

"Muzi, don't worry any more. I'll definitely arrange something for you to sedate your feelings and thoughts", Thenjiwe offers. I look at Thulani, and he looks away again.

Thenjiwe switches our focus to her stay overseas, "Life has not been rosy for me out there in the UK. For example, one chilly evening whilst l was just strolling on the streets for fun some overzealous police pounced on me. And accused me of soliciting sexually. The next thing I was handed down a deportation order. Do l look like a street walker, gentlemen?"

The rhetoric question gets me taking a slow swallow while swinging my head back and forth and saying to myself: Cut the crap, street walkers are not identified by words or some uniform they wear but by their actions. On that score, all credit goes to the British police for arresting a law-breaking dull-looking wanderer who was not going to give her clients value for their money anyway!

She continues:" I came back home. Then a year later l flew out and landed in Canada. l landed myself a somehow lucrative job as a personal secretary, but my boss would enter my office and say funny things like: you know what each time l look at you my biological clock ticks madly and l feel like winging away with you to Africa for good! And one day he pleaded with me to massage him because of sciatica. He was a good man. l couldn't rebuff his request just like that. And so l set out on rubbing him. The man started wheezing and screaming".

I cough for good measure, then start making a wincing gesture before quizzing, "Was this because of pain or was he convulsing because he had a certain disease?"

Thulani gnashes his teeth: "Nonsense! Of course he was moaning with pleasure."

Miss Hlahla downs another bottle, sends out a gust of groaning oral air before disclosing:" I was fired on the spot by the jealous wife!"

Now drunk and clear-cut like a disc jockey on a horse back, I comment, "For having clawed away some of the poor man's skin!"

Thulani blurts out, "Did you smoke weed? Don't be delusional and ridiculous, my girl is the most romantic soul alive. She's the cream of the cream!" I look at my friend as if to say: l see today you repose your faith in this stranger? All of a sudden I've become a crazy weed smoker to be yelled at in public? Whoever said women wield power and rule over men was not wrong. My friend seems to be worshiping this little woman! He must be wiping her backside with his fawning mouth these days. Shame, this is tragic!

After a few minutes have elapsed, I think to myself: People, indeed don't behave in the same manner under similar conditions unlike electrons, and I think because some fellows are simply morons, that's w hy!

Then aloud I ask her, "Are you a builder or what by profession?"

Ignoring the question Miss Hlahla continues: "In Canada l also worked in the bushes hacking off tree branches. The severe cold and the hazardous snakes and malaria eventually forced me to bid my workmates farewell".

"In Hungary one of my major tasks was to catch bats and rear bees for university researchers. But one researcher constantly made disingenuous derogatory remarks about the audacity of some people who fail to snitch out the sting of worn-out war criminals in the very backyards of their country and think they could somehow successfully and magically catch slippery bats in foreign lands!"

They say beer drives people to be frank and brave. I stand up and invite the two love birds,

"Sorry guys but this bat-catching thing does not look like a nice holidaying excursion even in front of my closed eyes! I think the people who were saying you should leave foreign bats alone were not wrong or mischievous. They meant to help a hapless bat-catcher! Let's dance and be blind to our problems as bats!"

But our dancing is short-lived…

A gigantic woman storms into the bar. She is breathing heavily like a racing athletic who seeks to outrun every competitor on the track.

Indeed she is determined to outsmart some people in the crowd.

It's Thulani's wife. "Loose woman, let me teach you a lesson you won't forget!" She grabs Miss Hlahla by her chin, and bangs her three times against the yellow-painted wall.

The poor girl collapses on the floor, her world is flighty. Her blood and vomit cascade on the floor, but my friend's wife is not through with her mission. She seizes Thenjiwe's miniskirt and in a matter of seconds it is screaming,"Creee! Creee! Creee!" as it tears apart. The small-figured lady is crying out for help and mercy as well. Were I not made to think she could sense danger and soar like an eagle? The crème de la crème of romance, power and intelligence?

Once done, she turns toward her husband. Is he about to confront his toughest marital test or this is a no-issue for my Women Affairs Mentor? Yes, Thulani who is the live wire, the mopani worm that vomits out on any person who touches it—is he about to diffuse a potentially embarrassing state of affairs? Yes, my close friend who does not take nonsense from any woman, has he set himself up for failure —or is he still up to the task? I watch for his reaction as the big-figured woman grabs her man by his very manhood, and hauls him out, much to the shock of the other revelers as well. What drama! I must be dreaming!!

I watch in horror as the man who has been giving me bold tips and advice on how to handle vocal women winces and hobbles into the dark. One female reveler remarks, "Oh that woman, she can surely castrate all empty male vessels who claim to be this and do that with her bare finger nails! That man howled like a beast facing imminent slaughter. Poor man, hope his manhood has not been uprooted by now".

The Immigrant With A Difference

Destiny

The New Year is heralded by wild and dramatic festivities: champagne toasts, fireworks, dancing, singing, and whistling. The people fill their champagne glasses to the brim with values and hopes, and they drink deep to the joy that the New Year can and should bring. They reflect and remember the previous year's feats and failures as they resolve themselves and look forward to the promise of a new start, a new year, a new outlook.

The most active-minded and celebrated holiday in the world has lost its meaning and lustre—that is as far as it relates to Sipho Mbongolo's life. Over the years he has taken stock and planned new courses of action, but all that has been unrewarding and frustrating. A life of losses and misses. That is the reality he sees. Even his weary gait and stance are evidence of his failures, so deeply have his conditions pervaded his thoughts and beliefs: has his slouch made his poverty, or his poverty his slouch, he wonders.

He has lost track of most of his childhood friends. He no longer knows where they vanished to. Did they disappear into the country's exodus crisis? Like quite a lot of his contemporaries and compatriots, maybe they migrated to the U.K., South Africa, Botswana, Namibia, U.S.—you name it. Any livable land, even a war-torn one, seems to be habitable, for that matter. All are in search of greener pastures. Do people not say there is a little Zimbabwe camouflaged in some parts of the U.K.? He knows it is a mirage beckoning him there, let alone becoming a British citizen. He always comforts himself: *We can't all be British*. He wonders without end why people fought frantically against his country's biased system, only to follow their enemies in the U.K. He is conflicted, but he is not confused by the country's socio-economic chaos. The ideals of the liberation war are lost on its perpetrators. "Independence" is like a fairy tale he'd once heard of. It is a lost cause too.

He wants to stay aware of time, but a sense of hopelessness has imprisoned him, like someone who binges on alcohol day and night. He has lost track of time; he has lost sense of time. He is oblivious to passing time, for time waits for no man. He is worried, for no man lives twice. Unschooled, unknown, and untraveled, what odds and opportunities does he have? What does the future hold for him? What is in store for him?

It is on the eve of the New Year that Sipho Mbongolo sets out on a journey to Bulawayo. As far as he is concerned, heeding Mzwakhe's call could be synonymous with a bold walk into his destiny. His cousin, Mzwakhe, has invited him to the big city, affectionately known as the City of Kings and Queens, to try out his luck in a bid to eke out a better living. Indeed, the New Year is a time for reflections and resolutions, a moment to recommit oneself to the causes and ideals one holds dear. For Sipho Mbongolo, a youthful, bucolic citizen, that moment of happiness, positivity, and celebration in his corruption-ravaged country has sadly become a mere transition from one day to the next. It is something he finds hard to hold so much significance for. *Time.* He has lost sense of time. Yet time is a reminder that the clock is uninterruptedly going *tick-tock*, that life is not stagnant, and that it's too short to be unlived and unnoticed. He is merely *existing*, and time seems to overlook his existence. Is time, like everything else, not felt and appreciated by those who *live*?

If Bulawayo is where his call of destiny is expected to manifest itself, or to be unlocked, or to be walked into, then once again time has made a mockery of his hopes and efforts, at least for a period of six months' wandering, wondering, and languishing before he bumps into Lady Mumba. In his heart, he is on the verge of going back to the rural areas when the unexpected happens.

***

Monday

Lady Mumba won't look Sipho in the eye. "How old are you?" Though it is not dark, the pupils of her eyes have been acting up, growing in size as if to provide her a clearer vision of the rustic man. "I'm t-twenty-f-five," Sipho responds in a rather shaky, strained voice.

"You're a man. Relax. What skills and experience do you have?"

"I can look at goats, cows, donkeys, cheap—I mean sh-sheep."

"Okay, you're good at looking after beasts. I wish I had a farm."

"What? Beasts! Bad things? No, I can't!" His astonishment is palpable and protesting.

"Livestock. Domestic animals. That's what I'm talking about." Lady Mumba titters.

"Sorry, sorry very much. I understand now."

This afternoon Lady Mumba is heavily hunched on an expensive-looking, fine-looking, gold-coated garden chair. Her huge back is jiggling and wiggling as if itchy, or as if balking at something bumpy or spikey. *How could such a magnificent chair be needle-like as well?* Sipho wonders, thinking of his father's stool that had been forbidden for children, treated as if it were spear-shaped. Actually, he'd been told of that chair, *No other ass, big or small, ever rested on it, not even the rude asses of tired or fussy visitors and relatives.*

"Sipho, with whom do you live in Old Magwegwe?" So short are Lady Mumba's lacy shorts that Sipho's eyes are magnetically riveted to where her enormous legs are joined together in a union of fat and flesh. The sight drives Sipho's poor heart into a series of emotional jerks. She still cannot look at him directly, but as if that emotional unrest is not enough distress for Sipho, she launches light and frisky kicks onto his lap, and his chest in turn vibrates breathlessly as the hormones really run riot. He drowns deeper and deeper in a pool of emotive and explosive agitation.

"Ah . . . ah . . . Madam Mumba, I sit with my small father, my small mother, and their children: Makhi, Mzwakhe, and

Sethekeli."

"Sipho, please call me Mona or Monalisa. Are your cousins friendly to you; do you get along well?"

Sipho's bloodshot eyes roll in their sockets, as if all they seek in this tempting world is to flee.

"They have the stubbornness of a black millipede—largely Sethekeli, who has no shame to say she cannot be under a man. She has a mouth, and I always protect her when her brothers want to beat her. But she thanks me by counting for me: hey I eat too much, hey I finish everything she gives, hey this, hey that. She has a tongue too.

That's why I don't tell her my secrets: because her chest was kicked by a zebra. She sees me quiet and thinks I have no liver to tell her not talk bad about me."

Madam Mumba cannot help laughing hysterically. "She has a mouth! A big mouth! A tongue? Well, she criticizes you baselessly. But what does a person who 'has a liver' do?

We all have a liver, don't we?"

"No, some people don't have a liver. Those who don't have the encouragement to tell you have a mistake. I have a liver. Even if I see a lion, I don't urinate with fear. I face it like uShaka!"

"You mean 'courage'! I see, but what do you mean your cousin 'counts for you'? You cannot count money?"

"No, I can. She *counts for me. Uyangibalela ukudla*. She says to people I eat too much of her father's food. She forgets tomorrow is yesterday." Tomorrow is yesterday. Time moves on. You can laugh at someone else's abject poverty today, but when you are in need in future, you may turn to the same person for help.

Lady Mumba's ribs are itching from a bursting of laughter.

She steadies herself, before tapping Sipho in a playfully hooking and tickling manner between his legs. The rustically man draws away, batting his eye.

He gasps, looks askance—much to the amusement of the teaser. She picks up a glass of wine and ungracefully some splashes out, dropping on her fatty neck.

"Sipho, you talk of your uncle, aunt, and cousins; where is your biological father? Ehmm. But before you respond to that question, please towel the split wine on my neck with your tongue." Sipho's yellow-tainted teeth are bared. If he were swimming, one would be forgiven for thinking that he were on the verge of drowning, for he is practically gasping for breath.

"My bio-o-logical father, he died five years old while the maize was kicking and the pumpkins were vomiting in the fields." His face is a little gloomy. He adds, "It was the disappearance of luck, as elders say. He, my father, didn't like a person who doesn't hear. His stomach was running him, running him . . ."

"Sipho, my goodness, you're such a fascinating literal translator. Your parlance is what is sometimes referred to as Ndenglish. I guess that even if you cannot give me a blowby-blow account of how your father died five years ago, you're basically saying he died while the maize plants and pumpkins

were blooming, or tasseling. Is that so?" The reply is phrased like a question.

"Yes—madam. No—Mona. Yes, is that so, shuwa. M-Mona,

I mean, he was going outside fast-fast. He was carrying heavy."

Lady Mumba tells him that life is a journey and a lesson on which trials and tribulations can be transformed into triumphs, brokenness into blessings. She concludes, "I believe in elevating and motivating others. Some people look for the rays of light instead of becoming the sunlight themselves." Sipho is enthused.

Outside, out of sight, she walks around, sneakily sprinkling salt all over the yard. Time tears on.

* * *

Wednesday Night

His bladder threatens to split apart with sudden violence if Sipho does not respond to the call of nature right away. To end up wetting the bed would be like a crime. How would he live with himself? He slips out of the double bed and blazes towards the door, hitting against the frame and cursing, "Demedi!" Common sense orders him to put on the lights. The lights uncover one thing: he is wearing a tattered undergarment, but he does not care a dot because he is alone. He slips into a pair of purple trousers and races into the toilet. Inside the beautifully painted, small room, he feels for the zip like an inept, butter-fingered fellow.

"Demedi! Where is the damn zip?" The zip—it is the other way round, at the back! He struggles with the waistline, hitches the trousers down, but no, the urine is irrepressible. Tremulously, he navigates his irritated human hosepipe to face the toilet pan—but the urinary stream just sprays and is hard to aim! It is already too little too fast. There is a desperate whirlwind inside him. It is spurting out, making the floor messy and cloudy. The short bursts of the coloured, watery waste have made an emergency landing on an exclusive imported tapestry.

The mess looks him in the eye as if saying: *I'm having the last laugh in my bubble bath*. He glares at it. At his hosepipe too. It looks innocent, stress-free, calm and collected now. He calms down after having relieved himself. Like an efficient scrub-man, he fetches the scrubbing cloth, sorts out his mess, and sighs the sigh of a fireman who has stumbled and fumbled before putting out a raging fire. He walks along the passage.

At Madam Mumba's door, he hears vocal noises. Sipho wonders, *Mumba dreaming aloud? Is she soliloquizing?* He places an ear on the lock set.

"I care for you."

(An inaudible sound.)

"Yes, I confess I was going out with that minister, but . . ."

(An inaudible sound.)

"Please, let's not dwell on that issue. You killed him out of jealousy, now you suspect I am going out with that . . ."

(An inaudible sound.)

"I won't shut up! I don't have a crush on him. He is just my .. . eh . . ."

(An inaudible sound.)

Sipho says to himself, *I am convinced that Lady Mumba is arguing with a boyfriend. Hmm, so she has a boyfriend after all.*

Anyway, she is only human.

Once in bed, he recalls how he ended up here. How last Saturday he met Lady Mumba in a salt queue, his speechless admiration for her high-class car. How a naked man burst into the queue and started fondling the backside of a plump woman,

who upon discovering the presence of the mentally challenged man, took to her heels like her body was a mere feather. How they talked about the incident and the endless queues, ending up discussing the sad state of the economy, and how Lady Mumba was prepared to dig him out of his financial mess by offering him a job as her bodyguard. How they later weaved their way through the bustling crowd into her gleaming car. How she said to him, "There will come a time when you will protect me in every way possible. When that time comes, both of us will happy. I will be happy. You will be happy."

Then on Monday, at what appeared like a billionaire's evening party, how at the Mumba residence, men and women who drove the latest and most expensive cars, spoke on the trendiest of cell phones, and wore immaculate designer suits converged, wined, and dined. They swayed in an English way and even sneezed in English—or so it seemed to Sipho. He remembers one silly man with an elephantine neck who gave him a glass of wine, and when he told him that he was a teetotaler and a member of the Zionist Bakhonzi Beqiniso Church, the man with a heavy neck called him a stupid, rustic pumpkin who did not know that heaven is on Earth.

He also has a vivid picture of a lady who told him squarely, "I love you boy. I've gold and silver. Gold is my first name. Fun my second. Body-luscious my surname. What more can a soul want? Those who have had the privilege and pleasure of rubbing shoulders with me have confessed that I uniquely nurture a soul's heart and body, as if the earth's axis is on my palm. Run away from this portly pig, Mumba. I would pay you more, give you my everything, boy. Just bring your freaking fresh figure to my place, boy. My body oozes love and more love for you. Your body, oh boy, I feel like licking you up like a chocolate bar. Please make me feel like a girl again?"

He remembers his response, telling this forward woman he'd already made marriage proposal to someone:

"I appeared for my wife some time ago. The go-between asked for a fire. I paid the open-the-mouth money. I will pay the suitor-be-known money. Sorry, besides in my culture, a woman does not smoke or point a man."

The smoking, swaying, and over-embellished woman unleashed F-prefixed obscenities at him. She called him the most unintelligent, rural, backward cat she had ever seen, before reeling away and canoodling a man who could easily have been her youngest grandson.

He is now half-asleep. He hears some patting sounds from a distance, but finally he drifts into sleep. He has a grandparent of a nightmare. mare.

* * *

Thursday Morning

A CURIOUS MOMENT

Sipho is feasting his eyes on the furnishings in the living room. He is gazing in awe at the fittings: an exotic Lalique crystal coffee table, with its high quality and gorgeously detailed designs. His eyes fall on an end table, lamps, a chair, an ottoman, a neat bookshelf, and a T.V. and stereo system. The couches in the spacious room are enclosed in a pigmented leather that speaks of durability and resistance to soiling. The air has a chocolate-like taste and floral aroma. Lady Mumba and Sipho are savoring the exotic Ethiopian coffee.

"That picture on the wall was taken some years back when I was in the U.K. Isn't it beautiful, Sipho?"

"It's beautiful, Lady—sorry, Mona. So you lived in the U.K.?" "For ten years. That's where I met some of the party attendees."

Sipho hops into a different subject.

"Madam, methinks there is a witch here?"

"What?" His boss grimaces, looking him in the eye, perhaps for the first time.

Sipho takes a mouthful of the coffee, as if he is unconscious of a tonal change.

"Methinks there's a witch who's doing rounds and sounds here. I hear them in the night."

"Sipho, get this clear: I hired a bodyguard, not a witchhunter."

"Sorry, madam, but I'm made to see in my dreams as a Zionist—"

"Antiquated nonsense! Whether you're a Zionist or whatnot, I don't bloody care a whit. Stick to your job description or else."

Maybe this subject is a no-go area. That is it. Madam Mumba is angry now. She is a flooded river. Maybe it is my fault? Maybe her boyfriend made her angry? Is he not loving? In Ndebele we say she is so angry she can swallow up a chameleon. Imagine the anger of a chameleon that has projected its long tongue. He too probably drives a stunning car. He must be one of the billionaires who were at the party.

Maybe he too returned from the U.K.? These billionaires, they will tell you they were once broke before they became billionaires!

These people have expensive things. They have lots and lots of money. If everlasting life could be bought, I think Lady Mumba and her billionaire friends would have bought it. People usually say life is not fair. However, I think the fairness of life is in that we breathe the same air, that we live and die no matter whether we are wealthy beyond description or poor in a sorry way. I think the difference is that people who have money enjoy because their lives are soft-soft, yet ours are hard like a rock.

Do they know the troubles of life? Life is harsh. These people live in their own world. A soft world that shines because of gold and silver. Most of them have soft bodies; they eat soft things, do soft jobs, shake with their soft hands, and sit on soft chairs. Who does not want to live in that world? I think these people have a good living. Poverty is a far-off thing to them. They probably do not know how it feels like to go for a day without a meal. I know it. It is my daily bread. I hum a little song or whistle, even if I walk into my crammed, small, dark bedroom. Once I get there, I sleep on the hard floor on my empty stomach and sometimes dream big dreams, dreams about having good things, soft things, peace, only to wake up and hear my stomach making funny sounds, complaining about emptiness, emptiness, and emptiness. I think their stomachs complain of too much different food, too much food, and too much food. Or maybe not. Their stomachs are used to it. That Monday evening, I ate many things with different colours, and my stomach, instead of celebrating, started behaving as if it had thunderstorms inside. My stomach made me shy because it was crying and crying in the presence of visitors. I am happy no one mentioned it.

Lady Mumba is dazzling in her dress. She shows him where to find food whenever he feels the pangs of hunger. After whispering, "Take care, I'll be back soon," she drives away.

* * *

Friday Evening

He has been searching for it high and low for almost five minutes to no avail. Has the T.V. remote control developed legs? He has no shred of doubt that an hour ago it was on the coffee table. His T.V. control remote skills have improved vastly since he came to Lady Mumba's residence. Tuesday was the day she taught him how to use a remote control, as well as how to start a car and a laptop. Lady Mumba has been kind and sometimes full of mischief and fun. Last Tuesday, did her right hand not stray all the way to the chubbiness and warmness of his lap when she was showing him how to operate the remote control? Did she not pat and pinch him on his waist? In the absence of a remote control, he gives up on watching T.V., but momentarily he dozes, trying to fight sleep off until he finally drifts into a slumber. On several occasions Sipho has slept through the noises and disruptions of stray dogs and donkeys in his dark hut in the village. He has always been regarded as a heavy sleeper by his family members in the countryside, but here, in this rhythm of weird footsteps, echoing screeches of windows, scratching of doors, howls of door fulcrums, and flipping of pages of books, his deep sleep deserts him and scurries for cover too.

always been regarded as a heavy sleeper by his family members in the countryside, but here, in this rhythm of weird footsteps, echoing screeches of windows, scratching of doors, howls of door fulcrums, and flipping of pages of books, his deep sleep deserts him and scurries for cover too.

* * *

7:55 p.m.

"Lady Mumba—sorry, Mona, are you back?"

Dozily, he looks around the room, but it is dark. *Who has turned off the lights? Is Lady Mumba playing games?* he wonders. *Wait a minute.* The orchestra of noises and goings-on dazes him. He feels unusually exhausted and uneasy. Daze and dizziness dance and conspire to hold him captive. He does not think it would be a good idea to stand up and make his way into his bedroom. He feels too shaky and too petrified to make a move. He wishes he had a blanket to bury and shrink his entire body under. If some mindless mosquito or louse were to nibble into him, he would not flinch. No body movement. No sound. If only he could be motionless—no yawning, no sneezing, no coughing, no burping—maybe the fear-provoking noises would subside. However, on the sofa his body betrays him because he cringes, yawns, sweats, sneezes, and freezes.

His body talks, twists, and toots.

Like an ostrich burying its head in the sand, he grabs three sofa cushions in a bid to shutter himself under them, but one slides away from him in the process. For what seems like an eternity, he tosses and turns on the sofa. Sleep is elusive. A fugitive. Now and then he kicks, lurches under a confused pile of interwoven sheets. *It is hunger or the heat? Or the cold air? Is it by virtue of the odd commotion? Is this a haunted house? Whose ghost? My dreams gave me an idea that there is something strange here. It is a ghost. I remember the conversation I overheard on Wednesday. Lady Mumba said, "You killed him out of jealousy, now you suspect I am going out with that . . ." This is perhaps the ghost of her former boyfriend. Yes. I'm no Shaka; if a hole were to open up, I would melt into it in no time.*

* * *

9:55 pm

Giddy, startled, and stuck, Sipho wishes the curtains could close on his nightmarish experiences. Nothing lasts. Happy times. Mourning times. Bad or good dreams. Any party will eventually come to an end. Good days never last, so neither should these bad moments. As if his prayers are being heeded and answered at that very moment, miraculously the lights come on, and the rhythm of footsteps echoing from the roof, the screeching of windows, scratching of doors, howling of door fulcrums, and turning over of pages of books all cease. He regains a little measure of physical, mental, and emotional stability, though drowsiness continues to take a toll on him. Obviously, he is relieved.

* * *

10:00 pm

Rats make noises while rolling nuts. Nonvocal noises. Rats and mice usually find refuge in lofts or ceiling cavities as they gnaw at electric cabling and other materials. Such interference with electric cabling can result in fires. Now no sounds reverberate and rumble on the roof. No rolling ball noises. *Maybe the noises were caused by small nocturnal creatures. Maybe there was no power*, he imagines. He prays that he does not spend a wakeful night. Sleep has made his eyelids as heavy as lead. His eyes are so sleepy that it is a challenge to keep them open. Nonetheless, he catches sight of the T.V. remote control. Dreamlike. It is back where he had left it! *No, that is something.* He wants to take a closer look at the remote control before laboring his way to his bedroom. Perhaps because he has been lying on the sofa for too or has some inflammation of the muscles, he finds it a bit difficult to get up from the sofa.

***

10:05 pm

Suddenly there is a high shriek of hinges and a sound as if someone has hit the main door with their knuckles. *Maybe the person outside does not know that the doorbell is not broken.* As if the night has not been difficult, distressful, and wearisome enough, Sipho's eyes fall on a small, terrifying gremlin, like a little humanoid bear. If he is drunk with sleepiness, he speedily sobers. The sight of it makes his hair stand on end. It has slithered into the room with neither a key nor a yanking open of the door. It seems like a dream. If it is a dream, something in the deep, dusky recess of his soul, he wants to be able to get out of it sooner than later. The glowing bloodshot eyes do not make matters better by their torching and torturing his mind. The sight of the hairy creature stabs his heart into palpitations, confusions, and tensions.

***

10:10 pm

Sipho studies the dwarf, with its radiant red eyes and long claws. It is approximately one meter in height. Its face would push both children and adults into freaked, dreamlike screams. It is attired in a wrap made of leopard skin and a neck-let of beads, little stones, feathers, and other strange bits and pieces. Around its waist there is a small bag. Sipho wonders what could be inside that pouch. *Maybe a knife?* It is in possession of a knobkerrie, too. *This is the dreaded tikoloshe*, concludes Sipho. A thought capers into his head. *Let me alert neighbors. A child who does not cry risks dying whilst strapped to the back of its mother,* so goes the wise Ndebele proverb.

* * *

10:20 pm

Sipho is like a badly injured, lily-livered soldier, who though has had a tortuous and agonizing journey, nevertheless is ready to soldier on, to summon strength and escape. He is not prepared to be kept prisoner for eternity by a creature rooted next to the main door, a creature that has not said what it wants. He straightens up, tries to open up his mouth to scream himself into a tizzy, but the tikoloshe is equal to the task. It swings at him in a flash and lands on his left shoulder. He can feel something heavy dangling there. Does it have a heavy, long tail? *Maybe it is an arm?* He can feel its head too. Nearly, it is a head the size of a huge water pumpkin. Its nose is a weird, snake-like sniffer, yet its ears are leaf-like in form. It attempts to slam him with the club, and he sees the knobkerrie hovering over his head, missing it by a few, lucky, anxious centimeters before it plummets.

With its long, emaciated legs and long claws, it tries to push and pin him down. Sipho rolls over the sofa, seeking to repel the creature with his tired arms. The human and gremlin wrestle and wheeze, call and curse. It clenches its teeth together tightly because of its anger and ego. The gritted teeth are all set to bite and chew off his right ear, as the hairy goblin's head is thrust on his body. Swiftly, it leaps up like a possessed mortal, before its sharp curved nails wedge into his neck, throttling him in the process. He winces. Like a defeated wrestler in the ring, Sipho is gasping, bleeding, pleading on the floor. The goblin lets out a throated chuckle.

* * *

Saturday Midnight

"People believe we, ze tikoloshes, are malevolent mythical elves of short statue zat pride in choking ze life out of zem! Well, you can see zat if one humbles oneself, like you did after regaining consciousness, we chat, we bear no malice, we make peace. We bury ze club!"

"Yes. Thank you, sir. I'm glad that your knobkerrie didn't smash my head into pulp".

The hobgoblin sneezes, sending out a yellowish, smallish, and circular fluid across the room. It patters on the ceiling. The little thing has jagged teeth. From a distance one could mistake it for a boy, not a grown man. Its skin is mottled and leathery. From their chat Sipho discovers some facts about the creature. For example, it is always a male, it has a single buttock, and it is known to be covered in hair or scales. It has hairy legs and feet. It is constantly barefoot. It is usually naked, but sometimes it wears a cloak. It wraps itself in the skin of a leopard or baboon when it is chilly. It speaks with a lisp. Its red eyes are capable of seeing well both in the dark and during the day. It does not have a tail. Sipho imagines, *How is it be possible that women can be attracted to such an ugly thing? Fine, it has strong, bony, and sharp fingers, and it is stout in build with a potbelly, but the face is very unpleasant, the skin shocking.*

"You are at liberty to ask anything about me." The tikoloshe's words cut into Sipho's thoughts. "You're stuck . . . no, stocky in build with a potbelly. What do you drink?" "Sorghum beer and sour milk".

"Is it true that you like moving into sleeping people's rooms and causing problems?"

"We can be visible and invisible at will. You can call us halfspirit, half-human. Hence, we derive pleasure from creeping into sleeping people's houses and scaring ze hell out of kids!"

It laughs out proudly and loudly. Its childlike voice is peppered with a swishing streak.

"There is a thought, rather a belief, that you are used for seducing women?"

"We've a mystic way of making women fall for us. A little charm.

I had a girlfriend who also worked for Mumba. 'Cause I'm a blast furnace in bed, ze maid left in a state of panic. But me finks she was already pregnant! 'Cause I'm a sharp shooter! I'm a red-hot iron. We've no match when it comes to sexual prowess. Shen . . . how can I put it? Shen, Mumba had no choice but to hook up wif me. Needless to say Mumba and I are an item. I'm a jealous, lascivious, and dangerous man. So very jealous zat you don't mess wif our relationship, by hook or crook, day or night, and live to see anozer day. Forget it!"

As if flaunting its weaponry, it paces around the room, carrying a manhood so long that it is slung over its own shoulder. Sipho is dumbstruck. What a sizable scrotum!

"Do you know the whereabouts of Lady Mumba?"

"I'm disappointed wif Lady Mumba. She won't get away wif it. I brought her all ze fortune she possesses and parades. Now she wants to get rid of me. Zat day she served me wif salty relish, yet she knows zat we're allergic to salt. She's spreading salt all over. I read ze mind. I visit ze sea. She forgets zat. Now she has left for Chiredzi, to seek a muthi man who will wipe me off ze face of ze earf. If my memory serves right, only one man of God has ever managed to kick me out of a house. Overwhelmed by his powerful prayers, I ran for dear life.

"Ze sangoma sinks zey can ward off a malicious spirit, exorcise ze area wif salt, charms, oil, and what-have-you? It's game on. Zis is set to be a battlefield. A titanic battle looms large. Bring it on. Ze sangoma must come over here prepared to put up a perfect fight, or else zey will faint, fall sick, or die. How narrow-minded! Kill me? Never! I killed her meddling minister boyfriend. I will kill her too if she continues running madly like a nervous fool trying to castrate a burly bull wif her bare teef!"

"How did you make Mumba reach?"

"Rich, you mean? I loot. Yes banks, factories, stores, mining concerns, you name zem—I raid."

* * *

Saturday 4:30 a.m.

Sipho cannot believe that in spite of his fears, trials, and weariness, he has been firing questions at the creature for so long and learning so much about it. He remembers the words of Lady Mumba: "There will come a time when you will protect me in every way possible. When that time comes, both of us will happy. I will be happy. You will be happy." He recalls that she added rather softly, "I hope you won't mind looking after me in my room when I ask you to, especially when I fall sick. Sipho, would that be a problem?" He'd been thrown speechless, tempted by a tenderness he now saw was never there. *I will ask one more question and avoid thinking about what Lady Mumba said, or else this creature will read my mind, and I'll get into trouble again.*

He wonders how much trouble Lady Mumba is in with this creature. "Madam Mumba will point the house where there is beer?" he asks, in his country colloquialism.

"Yes, zat woman will taste my wrath. They don't call me Ntokoloshe for noffing".

The dwarf disappears into Lady Mumba's bedroom, before emerging a short while later with a container.

"Listen, it's time for you to strike gold. Now take zis and disappear. Don't ever come back here. You did not talk wif me. You did not see me, is zat right? You disclose, you're dead. Zat me!"

Sipho cannot believe it. A suitcase filled to the brim with crisp notes! U.S. dollars. He walks past the colourful, computerised gate. With a trembling joy, he hurries on, his horizon characterized by the diminishing grandeur of the house and the snowballing mysteries inside. Let the soft lady solve her problems with her own soft hands. He could make his own future.

THE CONVERSE HOLDS TRUE

Thulani and Thethelela were very good friends before the fracas. These two boys owned a cow .Yes they owned a fat cow until fantasy proved to be a dense gimmick.

Yes they did or so they thought that was their deed. They decided to do what others did by buying lottery tickets indeed.

They shouted and argued together. They were at odds with each other over the size of the cow and over the apportioning of its part, over the ownership rights. A fight ensured. it dragged on and even sizzled while lottery results fizzled out unannounced and unknown.

A passer-by roped himself in .Thulani said the fight was about the ownership of legs.The intervener asked, "What legs?"

"Legs of a cow", was the reply

"Where is the cow currently?"

"Not here," chorused the boys

"Who actually owns the cow?"

"None", declared the boys in unison

The inquisitive passer-by was baffled as he battled with the root cause of their battle. The two scrawny scruffy boys had to explain in their anger fused and served with inanity. "We hoped to be winners and then later buy a fat cow but we disagreed on who would have the legs…"

THE HEN AND THE COCK

Once upon a time in a mineral-rich and landlocked country called Kudala lived a hen and a cock. They were the proud and progressive creators and owners of three shiny grass-thatched round mud huts that mesmerized and magnetized every passer-by as a spectacular sight. The couple had a truly beautiful home that was the envy of many a bird in a thick forest beyond a winding stream whose water always whispered and cascaded downwards with a rare musical calmness.

Some few years ago the two had bumped into each other at the stream in a wintry evening. Hen was heading homeward after fetching firewood whilst Cock was dejectedly bathing at the stream, as if trying to drown and wash away his sorrows and bad luck after a futile hunting adventure. Upon catching sight of Cock, Hen had attempted to eschew him or at best pass by silently and surreptitiously without him noticing her. However, Cock had other ideas. He greeted her in an earsplitting voice that startled her with a mixture of trepidation and bewilderment.

"How is your evening panning out?" She found herself asking him. She was somehow surprised at her own words. Was there a ventriloquist somewhere? How could she ask a stranger such a question? Where is the boldness and suddenness stemming from? She wondered.

"I ....I think things will look up for me. After all, my... .my evening is still a virgin". He responded with a stammer that seemed to betray his vain attempt at self- consolation and exaggerated steadiness. Deep in his heart, he was not convinced with his words. In fact, he was disappointed in himself and his response. How could he say things would look up when the entire world appeared as if it were on the verge of collapsing on him? Had his whole day not been anything else but a nightmare in the forest? While he was busy crucifying himself for what he saw as inappropriate wording, her parting words melted his state of dejection and self-accusation.

"Since your evening is still a little virgin, I'm sure by the time you are done with whatever you're doing, it would have lost its virginity many, many times!" He could not help but laugh hysterically. Hen's words were like a smart doctor's apt prescription for a dying patient. They magically injected a certain new lease of life into him-a heightened desire, an obligation and inspiration of being in charge of oneself, of being more than a hunter of food, but a humble seeker of committed companionship and life-long happiness. They left a pool of dazzling and invigorating thoughts that flooded his mind. A few days later the two birds met and chit-chatted. Before long they were hitting it out as the greatest of friends.

After going through the necessary cultural formalities, the two love-birds lived as husband and wife. It was not long before they populated their yard with ten chicks. Hen's motherly love was amazing and unquestionable. She always tried by all means to protect her hatchlings -coddling, cuddling and guiding them until they grew into little chicks that dogged her wherever she went. She kept an eagle eye on anything that came closer than necessary to her little darlings.

* * *

One day Eagle kept surveillance over Hen and her carefree chicks. He was spoiling for a blitz that would leave Hen flighty and her chicks in complete maze. The following day, his star shone and he pounced upon one chick. Nine chicks were left. Two days down the line, Eagle was at it again. He snapped up another chick. Cock and Hen were fidgety, furious and grief-stricken. How could such tragic losses come in thick and fast?

They then mapped out a strategy to counter Eagle's predatory tendencies. A week elapsed without an unfortunate incident being recorded. There was neither the disappearance nor devouring of a little chick. Time tore on. It looked like alarm bells were no longer ringing as loudly as before. However, as the dust was slowly settling down unfortunate crept in again. This was after Eagle had zoomed about majestically in the firmament before whizzing down and scooping up a dazed and fleeing chick. It was a tremulous and disconcerting experience for the chicks. All Hen and Cock could do was to helplessly watch Eagle scurry away, soar and disappear into the vastness of the sky with their dear blood and flesh.

Both were dumbfound and mournful. What would it take to provide an all-out security for their beloved chicks? They could not bear to imagine another possible loss of their loved chick to insatiable Eagle within the twinkling of an eye. Their hearts were worried and bleeding. It was clear that as long as Eagle loitered about, danger also lurked. They restrategised. The bird of prey tried to swoop on the chicks with ease and speed but each attempt seemed to fizzle out into an exercise in futility.

A CURIOUS MOMENT

Then there was a disturbing turn of events which took centre stage. Weather variations resulted in a long spell of drought. Cock as family head had to dutifully go hunting on a daily basis. Cock sought to fetch and prey on grasshoppers. In essence, he looked for anything edible, ranging from fruits and nuts to cockroaches. He hunted with great determination and diligence. He had to stave off starvation. However, more often than not, his hunting sprees did not bear fruit.

* * *

At home, Hen paced about in the yard, looking for bits and pieces to feed her chicks. The little ones darted about, competing for food and their mother's attention. Jealously she rendered maximum fortification and guidance. She played the role of protector and provider with a measure of distinction. She would tour the yard with her chicks until fatigue got the better of them. They would while away time under a thickly-branched orange tree. Her beak agape, she gasped and craned her neck, rarely dozing off, but on other stupid days she succumbed to one or two stubborn naps in the process. Waking up with a little fright and wonder, she would count her blessings upon discovering that her remaining nine chicks were still intact.

She could not elude one thing. Loneliness took its toll on her as Cock was wont to leave for the forest at dawn and arrive at home at dusk. It was a routine. One day neighbour Cock paid Hen a surprise and flying visit. Hen gave him a cold shoulder by virtue of the fact that her husband had categorically and strongly advised her to keep him at an arm's length. "If I had a choice, he wouldn't have been our neighbour. Dear partner, don't fall for his silly traps that could come in the form of kindness or smiles, or indeed, understanding or friendly visits, because, one thing for sure he always has ulterior motives. Under no circumstance should you entertain his overtures. Simply give him your back. Please keep him at bay. What he deserves is as wide a berth as the North Pole and the South Pole because he is cunning, envious, thievish and dangerous. In the same vein, to have an affinity with such a character is tantamount to having a relationship with a vicious bloodsucking mole or a snake in the grass", he had warned.

Each time Hen's eyes slapped on neighbour Cock, she bolted away and never looked back. However, neighbour Cock, being of persistent and persuasive nature, gave chase. Such was neighbour Cock, not despairing easily. It looked like his was a wild goose chase as each time neighbour Cock heaved in sight, Hen remembered the words of her husband : He is as sweet-tongued as a conman who can hoodwink one into offloading one's precious savings to him. He is so dangerous that he can sweet-talk any bird into selling its one and only pair of wings. Hence have absolutely nothing to do with such a charlatan and a mole because he can use any bait under the sun to achieve his evil aims and objectives. Beware.

***

One day Neighbour Cock, acting like a parent having a correlative duty of support, brought Hen and her chicks some grain of millet. Even if Hen ran away, looked away –with zeal and zest the hungry chicks helped themselves to the food neighbour Cock had left behind. They did not care whether it was a little loot ransacked from someone else's granary or field. All they wanted was food, nothing else. After neighbour Cock had disappeared, Hen, too, partook of the millet food. After all, she too was starved of food, and she too relished such a meal. Hen beseeched the chicks never to divulge to Cock about neighbour Cock's frequent visits, let alone his spirit of generosity, not monstrosity.

***

On the second day, Hen saw no point in running away upon seeing neighbour Cock. As the days tore on neighbour Cock decoyed her to sit next to him and before long they were chatting about many issues, including the devastating drought. He handed over some goodies to Hen, who in turn shared them with her grateful chicks. Like a blind sycophant, neighbour Cock used every opportunity available to shower praises upon Hen for being in the thick of things to ward off hunger, disease and misery; something typical of a truly loving mother to her chicks. He even patted her on her back for a job well done!

Neighbour Cock managed to endear himself to the chicks by virtue of his fatherly cheerfulness, generosity, humorousness, charm and diplomacy. "He is not harmful but wonderful.

What a friendly, jocose and kind neighbour we have, mum, "remarked one enraptured chick to Hen one morning as neighbour Cock was disappearing into the thickness of the forest after giving them a dozen of lean grasshoppers. For Hen, the chick's statement was an assurance that her husband would not be posted on what transpired behind his back. She reiterated that as long as their father did not glean any information about neighbour Cock's compassion towards them, starvation would be a thing of the past.

***

One Monday afternoon Hen weaved her way with verve to neighbour Cock's homestead at the invitation of the latter. She was convinced that their neighbour was an enthralling and caring man whose corns they could not afford to tread upon. In fact, his exuberant voice was music that had grown on her. That day she brought her chicks a small bag of tasty groundnuts. They feasted on them happily. The following morning neighbour Cock made his way to their homestead and they spent the better part of the day playing a chase-andcatch game with Hen. They ran, laughed, joked and tucked into a delicacy together like they had known each other for ages. She found neighbour Cock vivacious, their time spent together delicious.

Neighbour Cock had bid them farewell after a day well-spent when he inadvertently stepped on an ashen chick that was sleepy. " Haaa this is so painful that it cannot go unreported. I'll definitely tell my father". All Hell broke loose as in cold blood; neighbour Cock strangled that grey chick to death with a startling suddenness that left Hen shell-shocked. He slammed the behaviour of the little chick, whose innocent body lay cold, inanimate and silent. Hen was inarticulate with fury, profound melancholy and forlornness. She was silently wondering: What monstrosity is this? What brutality is this? Where is the conscience of neighbour Cock in this act of madness and vileness? All along were his smiles and kind gestures a mere gimmick? A death trap? Why didn't l see all this coming? Why did l allow a heartless snake to sneak into my life? Why have l allowed myself to be an accomplice in the blood-curdling killing of my dear chick? How am l going to live with this guilt? I rue the day l yielded to his stratagem.

Why did l do such a foolish thing? Why?

"This chick died at the venom of a waylaying snake. Cock should never ever get wind of anything else other than this version. Am l making myself clear?" Neighbour Cock roared rhetorically beyond remorse. Hen's gait lacked elegance as she staggered, carrying the lifeless body of her chick. She faltered clumsily as she entered the biggest of their three huts which was used as a bedroom. A cloud of sorrow and petrification enveloped her, galvanizing her into studying and caressing the motionless body of the chick. She was sobbing uncontrollably when Cock strode into the room. He was told that their chick was lifeless owing to a certain merciless snake's wicked deed. Needless to say Cock was crestfallen and confused. After that tragic incident Neighbour Cock vowed never to set foot on the yard of Hen and Cock.

* * *

One rare Sunday evening Cock came home rather early. He was carrying a big brown fruit that looked appetizing. "This wild fruit is a beauty. The moment l laid my eyes on it, l knew that it was potentially our windfall. However, we need to be more careful lest it becomes our catastrophic pitfall. We all have one life to live. What l mean is that the suitability of this mouth-watering fruit for consumption is questionable. At face value, it looks harmless, but we would be exhibiting a terrible height of folly if were to gobble it up without ascertaining whether it is fit for consumption or not. I therefore suggest we give Rat a little piece of that fruit and see what happens. This shouldn't be interpreted as an act of cowardice and cruelty. Not at all. That move will serve as our control experiment, "giggled Cock in a prematurely victorious fashion.

Rat was appreciative and prayerful. He promptly and hungrily tucked into the piece. Cock and Hen waited for a possible abdominal war to be waged. Thirty suspenseful minutes elapsed. An hour lapsed. Time tore on. Rat did not complain of something amiss in his stomach. All is well that ends well, thought Cock. Three hours later the family could not wait any longer. They enthusiastically consumed the aromatic and delicately-textured fruit. The entire family ate their fill. Hen and Cock chatted, patted and joked with a passion of its own life. Their world was abuzz with laughter, dance, song and humour. They had not celebrated as a family before. Cock felt liked a feted hero in his homestead. They even renewed their pledges of loyalty and love to each other in grand style.

Dove shot in and expressed her heart-felt grief over the fate of Rat who lay lifeless a few meters from the nearby stream. What! Faces fell with apprehension. They knew what that information meant. Both Cock and Hen individually decided to do something before the effects of the deadly fruit finished with them. What had befallen Rat was surely waiting for them. What a prospect! Cock fidgeted about, whispering a seemingly endless inaudible prayer. After a while, Hen, as if at a confessional, divulged, "l hereby confess that because of my follies and failings l allowed neighbour Cock to visit me. His persistent, sugarcoated words became my daily food. Words, like swords-can spear one's heart into divisions. Contrary to what l told you, it was not a snake that killed our chick. Neighbour Cock took the life of our dear chick. He used to give me many irresistible gifts in the form of food. They say one good favour deserves another. I'd be lying if l said l didn't enjoy many favours. In a you- scratch- my- back- l -scratch -yours gesture I reciprocated those favours. I am sincerely sorry for those iniquities and stupidities; please forgive me before we depart yonder".

To her surprise, Cock unequivocally and unconditionally agreed to forgive her. "I also transgressed full-time. Your follies and failings cannot exonerate me. For example, one day during my hunting sprees l couldn't catch a thing, and on my way home l bumped into a little cute hen who said her entire family had perished at the teeth of a vicious dog. She claimed to be lonely and looking. She gave me a flabby grasshopper, and shy of coming home empty-handed, l accepted the offer. Little did l know that she would end up being my chatty and chortling companion. That's why l was away from dawn to dusk. We embarked on many captivating hunting sprees. As if that were not enough, I also fraternized and gallivanted with several birds of dubious character. I was promiscuous and imprudent. In modesty and earnest, I admit in your respectful and respectable wifely presence that such deeds were totally superfluous and iniquitous. I'm truly sorry for plunging our sacred union in mud. Now l know that anyone who is unforgiving is done for. Indeed, to err is human, to forgive divine.

Please forgive me before the world falls on us. Please, please forgive me". He pleaded nervously. It was as if his middle name was Meekness.

As soon as Hen had pronounced, "Forgiven utterly", Rat entered the room. To their awe, Rat was alive and well. How come! He explained that after partaking of the delicious fruit, he had slumbered in a blissful and inspirational manner like one in a paradise for the privileged few. Meanwhile, Cock angrily and arrogantly dragged Hen to another room to fully elucidate what she had just mentioned about neighbour Cock's frequent visits, the nature of their relationship and the circumstances leading to the demise of their chick." You have some serious explaining to do. If you aren't the mother of my chicks, then you'll get away with this comedy of errors I don't find amusing. If you're, then you're doomed", he threatened.

Cock was no longer himself. Rage had captured, blinded and imprisoned him. It was as if he did not have shock absorbers, or if he had them, then they were either dysfunctional or were playing up. Hen's heart was skidding and pounding with a life of its own. In spite of her obvious fears and confusion, at the back of her mind, she pictured their world hurtling down to Mother Earth. For her, it was a time to gain an insight into who really they were and since they could not undo their past, she saw it as an opportunity to reflect on and learn from their experiences and errors. It had to be the moment of truth…

OFFICE DRAMA

If Mrs. Vithikazi Nhlaba had never considered herself a jealous wife, she certainly made herself one after darting into the Human Resources Manager's office only–Good Heavens—to find Miss Simo Mahlangu, the usually calm and shy company secretary, sniggering and posturing below the very nose of Mr. Sinothi Nhlaba.

Long ago when Mrs. Nhlaba was a young wife, and had verbal bouts and tiffs with her husband over his lateness, her rustic aunt once said to her, "Don't raise eyebrows yet. Hold your peace. You're a woman who works hard like an ant bear. He can't afford to lose you if he has an ounce of brains in his head. Not maggots or termites. By the same token, you can't seek to kill a snake whilst it's still in its hole, lest there's no snake at all in the first place. Call to mind, our wise elders advised us against holding the flying ant by its head lest it flies off!" They also said: "What is horny cannot be hidden (forever). The truth will come out."

Mrs. Vithikazi Nhlaba respected her aunt, but her head was inundated with countless ideas and unanswered questions. Did her aunt board the bus all the way from EMaguswini to preach such an impossible gospel? Today, I'm traveling to Bulawayo to tell Vithikazi to be subservient to her husband. I might be rural, old and uneducated but I know how to handle wayward men. Did she ever give thought to what she was saying? For starters, was it humanly possible and easy not to be suspicious when one partner's concentration had clearly been swayed away? How could her aunt advise her to hold her peace in the face of such a shift? Was that shift not as bad as an act of betrayal? So she was expected to swallow up such nonsense unquestioningly because she worked like an ant bear? What if indeed he had maggots or termites for brains?

If her aunt put herself in her shoes for just a few days would she stand his strange behavior? After all, was she not her maternal aunt? Don't raise eyebrows. Hold your peace. How can peace be held when wars of disquiet are being waged against one? Was her husband not slipping away from her bit by bit? How could she not raise eyebrows when he was coming home late every night? And as if that were not enough headache on its own, without an explanation or word of greeting he would slump on the couch and sleep soundly? Was his seemingly blissful snoring from the living room not her series of nightmares? Did her aunt have any idea how emotionally disconcerting the whole experience was? How could the unenviable journey of wondering where her husband had been and what he had he been up to be an easy or peaceful one?

Hold your peace? Really? What peace? Did her aunt know that she was worried to death about his safety and well-being? For example, what if street thugs pounced on him at night, how would she live with herself and her self-denial? What if he had found omakhwapheni with whom he was spending the better part of the night, and were as usual, feeding him with food spiced with shovels and shovels of their zwanamina in a bid to crown him their toyboy? Hold your peace?

Still? Queries and thoughts assailed her mind, her peace, her days and nights. Maybe she was paranoid. Maybe she wanted to be practical. Was it her little cock-eyed illusions and delusions that the man she loved dearly was coming home late night in night out?

When her aunt, who to her best knowledge had been single since time immemorial, finally left for EMaguswini after a week's stay, Mrs. Nhlaba decided to seek further advice and guidance from a number of diverse spiritual sources.

"Do you know what kind of things dogs eat?" the man in a stuffy and small hut with an herbal air to it asked.

"I'm looking for a solution to my husband's truancy. Now I'm wondering: what have dogs and what they eat have to do with this problem?" queried Mrs. Nhlaba, trying to suppress a strong wave of impatience.

"Everything. You and I know that it has absolutely everything to do with those domestic animals. Madam. Men are..."

"Oh no, not that antiquated stereotypical stuff about men and dogs! "She found herself interjecting.

"But this is a fact of life, even our elders acknowledged that correlation, that comparison."

"Please, not all men are like that. For example, I've friends, relatives and neighbors whose husbands and boyfriends are consistently loving, faithful and well-behaved. Stop making dangerous comparisons, outmoded assumptions and conclusions."

"I thought we're talking specifically about your husband's actions, not about the lifestyles and behaviors of your friends, relatives or neighbors. I receive and attend to a lot of people from different walks of life every day. I know what I'm talking about. The last time I checked how most of men behaved, the results were the same. Men are..." The man wearing some awe-inspiring traditional regalia was in the process of defending his theory in a defiant, bold and boastful fashion when Mrs. Nhlaba interrupted him.

"Look, man, this is the 20th century. Rise from the dead and start to live again. Get a life and wake up. I can clearly see that your view of the modern world is retrogressive. It's reeling under a sick, old, parochial and patriarchal ego. You need help because you're a patient languishing from a terrible chronic ignorance. Let me tell you this for free: you've another thing coming if you're entertaining any single idea of ever convincing me that men are nothing else but dogs in disguise. You know what that's called? It's a lame, lousy and loud excuse for lacking true manly qualities. Last week I wasted my precious money and time funding the trip of my pastoral aunt from EMaguswini all the way to Bulawayo, hoping she would help me deal with my man's delinquency in a mature, fresh, and fair manner. Alas, it wasn't to be. Upon arriving, guess what, she categorically told me not to raise eyebrows, but to hold my peace. What audacity. What impetuosity. As if that were not enough joke, you've seen it fit to waste my cash and time. I've just paid a consultation fee here only to hear you harp on a silly and archaic connection between men and dogs. How does that solve my problem?"

She questioned rhetorically as she stormed out of the circular mud-walled, grass-thatched room, whose herbal odor had given her nostrils something to contend with. The traditionalist was startled by Mrs. Nhlaba's unceremonious departure. Undeterred, she sought the services of fortunetellers and traditional doctors like she was possessed, like they held the key to her happiness. It was as if they held the epicenter of her life and future in their concoctions, in their invocations, in their pronouncements and in their rituals, and even on their horizons and crystal balls.

"What's your husband's favorite food?" asked one female herbalist.

"He relishes isitshwala with okra or isitshwala with beef stew."

"Great! Then I've a panacea to your quagmire."

"What are you going to do?"

"Actually, the remedy lies with what you'll have to do."

"Really?"

"Yes. You should claim your husband back with your hands."

"How, doctor? Follow him like a shadow, and then drag him back home?"

"No. It's simpler than that. Your urine, saliva and lizards' tails will do the trick."

"You just need to follow the short procedures and prescriptions, and the man will rush back and fall at your feet, begging for forgiveness and love. The die will be cast. Don't you want to be his irresistible queen again?"

"Yes, I do. Mmm ...but my bodily excretions like urine and all...ngeke bantu! Honestly, my belief system, my conscience... both don't allow me to..."

"Madam, this is not about your religion. This is about finding a solution to your problem." She left in a huff.

** *

One day one confident and flamboyant prophet gave her what he called his never-failing anointed seawater, and vowed that in the next two days, Sinothi Nhlaba would be back in her warm arms as soon as he had knocked off from work. It was not to be. In essence in the following two days, Mr. Nhlaba bettered his past record of lateness by arriving home after 2:00 a.m. and 3:00 a.m. respectively. Mrs. Nhlaba's anxiety reached boiling points. She would dig into Mr. Nhlaba's pockets and briefcase with the hope of stumbling on some evidence to link it with his sluggishness to be home. There was no mark of feminine touch on his face, no sign of lipstick, except for his lazy eyes that rolled in their sockets each time he arrived.

It soon turned out that Mr. Nhlaba's unpunctuality was none other than the crazy result of his newly-found love—BEER. However, that day when she caught sight of Miss Mahlangu seeking to draw the attention of her husband like a magnet would a drawing pin, her aunt's words speared through her head before disappearing into obsoleteness. She concluded that Miss Mahlangu's intentions were far from being venial. She was a "devious temptress" playing her devilish cards in a dangerous fashion. Nothing more, nothing less.

As for Miss Mahlangu, she was comfortable and free in her garments. She was of the opinion that a number of rank marshals, drivers and touts were simply nosy, overzealous and judgmental. They had no business in heckling and harassing women over what ladies sported. Did those men have expertise in fashion? They did not look like persons of good taste, either. Far, far from being connoisseurs, at all. Personal hygiene was what they should have been minding. They fooled around as if they had great sensitivity to beauty, civility and culture. What rudeness! Most of them were total strangers to women on the streets. Women doing their business, minding their business. How dare those total strangers cross a line and go beyond accepted limits or standards of behavior. She vowed to put them in their proper p lace.

***

One Monday morning when she was alighting from a city cab, a tipsy emergency taxi tout had remarked, "You're like a twin cab limousine cruising to a palace, girl. Submarine maybe. A loaded bazooka doesn't come any close to this. A top jet-fighter! Yeah! I've not been to any airport in the world, but I think you fly beyond the furthest clouds, you cruise at 130,000 feet...whatever! Assets, is your middle name. If you were sweets, you would be a packet of chocolate. If you were a TV set, you would be that big plasma; I mean a big flat screen.

If you were music, you would be an LP, not a 7-single disc. No!

And if you were a bed, you would not be a double—you would be a queen! I want to crown you my beautiful big bumblebee baby. My beautiful queen. Tell me, how do I become the king caretaker of that beautiful wealth, eh? Please make me rich!"

That morning she decided to cough out her anger on the man.

"Nx! Who are you talking to, hopeless, manner-less drunkard?"

"Obvious, to you, big beautiful queen. How can you ask whether the goat is female or male when its back is facing you, baby?"

"Get the hell out of my sight. You must be a mentally sick dirty daydreamer. A walking dead thing. I'm not you type. OK? Fuck off, maan! A piece of discarded, smelly and tattered cloth!"

"Take it easy. Easy. You're right 101 percent. I'm sick. I have amatheketheke in my veins, in my body. Once I remove them, and get umvunsankunzi from ikhehla from edladleni, I swear I will be grand and back for you. Shame. There will be thunder without rain! Hehehehe, I'm Mr. Mkhonto, for your own information. That's my nickname. I can sense a beautiful lady from a distance. Suppose you're on the fiftieth floor, coming down in an elevator for queens and beauties and I'm on the first floor, I can tell with my eyes closed that you're landing down, girl. That's me! My heart's hooter is blowing and going: LOVE HELP ME, LOVE HOLD ONTO ME, LOVE FLY WITH MEEE PLEASEEEE!!! I can feel your presence like a good computer detecting a WIFI router. That's me! In fact, I've a special love wireless extender in my body that makes me see you from afar! There's a good connection between you and me. Listen to your heart now. Love has no type, no class, no size because it is blind. Do you catch me there? I think you were born for me, and that you're my kind of cow, you know. Don't say I am a piece of tattered cloth. I am helpful. I help drivers and commuters. I am connected.

You don't know that if you become my queen you will have free rides every day because I know all the kombi drivers here. You will have fresh eggs, cheese, steak, macimbi, pies, pizza, ox-tails and tongues of fat cattle, legs and wings of proper chickens from the rural areas and all the choice meat you can dream and think of every day. Not the tasteless chicks you see around here. Maybe you talk like a high-class official, yet you chew vegetables every day like a rabbit. That will be a thing of the past. I know all the butcher men in the city centre. Let's not talk about my job. Let us talk about our future. Let me oil my engine.... Sting. Sting. You will see. Boom! Explosions. Boom! Explosions. Mngci. Mng ci..."

Her claim as a fighter for her rights, though not completely immune from street obscenities—coupled with her dress code was a bold statement about yearning for a certain feminine freedom, dignity and expression. Of course, many a careless and salivating man had used her skimpy dress code as an excuse to feel the immensity, elasticity, and gentleness of her ample backside. No surprise, then, that she had hurled some unscrupulous men to the courts of law or rained scorching slaps and fists upon them.

When Mrs. Nhlaba unceremoniously walked into her husband's office, to her shock and surprise, Miss Mahlangu was strategically bent over a small cabinet file, her sky-blue minidress revealing a diaphanous, multicolored undergarment that left little to the imagination. Mr. Nhlaba considered himself as being physiologically normal. No matter how he tried to look away from Miss Mahlangu's backside, he found his rather dizzy glances falling on her, the whole sight playing a game of electricity with his unsuspecting hormones. His body was battling internally with a certain tempting chemistry he loved to hate.

In SiNdebele, they say eyes are so insatiable they cannot be served with enough food, meaning that even if one told himself to look away from something or someone, more often than not, curious eyes tend to be stubborn and misleading. As hard as he tried to look away, his gaze riveted to Miss Mahlangu when Mrs. Nhlaba lurked about like a cornered snake.

Mr. Nhlaba's wife was not prone to being at the centre of various office imbroglios, but she felt obliged to act on what she considered to be her husband's secretary seductive ploy and antics. She had to nip such wayward behavior in the bud, or else she would remain holding to a little feather when the bird had slipped through her clasped hands. The way her husband's eyes seemed to feast on Miss Mahlangu backside made Mrs. Nhlaba insecure and suspicious.

Mrs. Nhlaba used to have a big frame when she was a child. In her twenties, because of the constant hype about the beauty of a slender body promoted and propounded by glossy magazine lifestyle editors and several local and international tabloids, she jumped into a dieting regime. Her daily gym sessions worked wonders as she shed kilos and kilos over a period of six months until she was a lean young beauty. She met her husband Sinothi at the Luveve Gym Trim Centre, who would later shower praises upon her. Then when they started dating, he called her his SSPP, an acronym for Sweet Slender Portable Possession.

"What the heck do you think you're doing, Simo?"

"I'm doing my work?"

"Naked?"

"Your eyes must be deceiving you!"

"Don't be silly, what are you trying to achieve?"

"To meet today's aims and objectives in the most efficient and effective way."

unfolded like a plot in their midst. Hare suffered a series of fall-outs with friends and other animals the moment he acted and thought of himself as the centre of the jungle. When other animals, old or young, counseled him, he closed his ears with stubs in a condescending fashion, declaring to himself that they were noisy nosy fools. On those occasions, he would get up from one of his kingly and gold-coated chairs he had won year in year out, and would swagger towards the counselor, cough once or twice for good measure and rhetorically ask, "What have you just said?"

Then he would ensconce on his raised grass -and -leafcushioned bed, then roll and dance on it without a care in the world. He would let out an obviously forced and elongated laughter, declaring that he had run his eyes over the breadth and width of the forest and had not seen any single animal worthy and capable of outrunning him even during his sleepiest and weakest moments. Not in his lifetime, no animal, no insect, no reptile, no bird should delude himself or herself of taking the crown away from him, he swore boastfully. No animal, no insect, no reptile, no bird deserved to sit at that throne. He forgot the old African adage: the words of an elder do not fall down into thin air.

A clean braggart, Hare had treated most of the entire forest's animals like dirt and rags. His heinous escapades were known throughout the forest. He was infamous because his claws dripped with the blood of innocent animates. With his unbounded pride, cruelty and deceit he thought he was beyond reproof. Therefore, the sweet victory of Tortoise over Hare threw the entire jungle into wild celebrations characterized by whistling, ululation and dancing never known before. The rains pounded the forest in an unprecedented way, too. The leaves of the trees gaily waved at the celebrants. The grass smiled with renewed life and liveliness. The birds chirped, soared and whispered among themselves with an amazing jollity, marveling at the wonder of wonders. The reptiles waltzed and waggled about with excitement.

The groups were many and various beyond count. They seemed to be in the seventh heaven of happiness. For example, there was an army of ants and caterpillars ,a herd of buffalo and antelope , a brood of chickens, a litter of cubs, a cowardice of curs, a clowder of cats, a quiver of cobras and an intrusion of cockroaches, all crowning the entire gathering a beauty of diversity . It was a bustle and hustle. A colourful hive of activity, it was. Indeed the forest was intoxicated with the newly found glee of freedom, hope and unity.

Peacock in her many colours swayed and strutted like a comedian. Dove hugged her with her loving wings. "Guess who is here-compatriots and friends? Who has joined the party? Yes, the queen of all flashy snobs and fakes. Oops! She's here to spoil our coveted party with her sickening colours and conceit!"Carped Eagle. Duck hobbled about and squeaked, "She's welcome. We're different and beautiful, please let us learn to embrace one another with unconditional love like Dove. Queen Peacock symbolizes the colours of the rainbow, the diversity of our paradise, the rich forest bestowed upon us by the Supreme Being. What can be more beautiful than that? Nothing". Queen Bee concurred, her protruding back was wiggling in majestic concentration.

On that day, Hyena, a nocturnal drifter heaved in sight. So did Owl. Ngcethe, the smallest bird in the vicinity, immediately flew off and landed on the neck of Hyena, and before any one animal or bird or insect could ask what was the matter with Ngcethe, he had nestled on the head of Owl.

In fact, he soiled Owl's head with great generosity. When asked about the reason behind his antics, he chortled", Wee! Wee! Wee! They say night is right for their naughty acts. These two are comrades in night crimes! We don't sleep because of their night craft!"

Lion roared," No, this is not the time for witch-hunting. Whether these comrades embark on nocturnal sprees or not is neither here nor there. This is not the time to fuel hostilities. This is our carnival, our victory against degradation, our time of freedom. This is the time to bury our differences of the past, and restore dignity and fair play for sake of the present and the future. We are starting on a new page and a new chapter. We therefore call for unity in diversity; we emphasize and preach tolerance and forgiveness. We cannot consolidate the fruits of our freedom and peace with petty squabbles. Let us demonstrate the spirit of love and respect. Even Hen shouldn't entertain an idea of ever swallowing up Locust one day no matter how ravenous for that tender meat she is. No. We seek actions and words that contribute to our collective development. We seek efforts that will promote our thrust towards civilization. There's a mammoth task ahead of all of us. We have to be level-minded and to revive the spirit of togetherness for our betterment. We have to rebuild where there is a signature of destruction, bring hope where there is despondency, and render security where there is danger. Change mindsets, challenge stereotypes and chart out the way towards total emancipation and active participation irrespective of whether one is a bird, insect, animal or reptile and so on.

In the true spirit of love, peace and progress, let me say this in a humble way, we're now friends, brothers and sisters. By the same token, I mean in the spirit of fairness, we're all equal and worthy of utmost love, respect and protection.

However, the same cannot be said for Hare and Elephant. I know that Hare's patently embarrassing defeat has come as quite a shock for Elephant. Honestly, in life, whenever one is taking others for granted, the hour of judgment is always coming. It does not matter how long it takes. It does not matter how slippery one is. The moment of truth is always on the doorway, ready to knock and unmask someone's age-long lies, follies and fallings. Just like the hour of our demise. It is always nearing, and rearing its head.

It is easy for the axe which hacks off the tree, to forget about its wanton act, but the tree cannot forget. To this end, we've been clear and unanimous in that the twosome sow seeds of destruction, trepidation and hatred. To this end, dark or blue, the twosome has to account for their actions and decisions. They have made their bed, they just have to lie on it. They have to explain to us what they did and for what reason they did whatever they did. They cannot harvest oranges of life and love, if they sow poison. Not at all. He who puts a seed of death in the soil, cannot expect to reap a fruit of life. It's as basic as that. If those two felons walk scot free a cow will certainly give birth to a person in Mhlanhlandlela!

My father will resurrect and storm out of the grave and demand justice! I swear with my own father who was tricked into holding on to a boulder by Hare until tiredness took its toll on him, and eventually the rock crushed him to death. I am an orphan but he is still around and alive, and ready to do much more harm. No. Simply No. Hare has always deluded himself that he monopolizes wisdom and power. The time of reckoning is upon us. What does not end is portentous, our elders aptly said. What flies, no matter high, at one time or the other does what? Yes, it will land on the surface. There is no wiseacre who licked their own back, our seniors cautioned. Woe to Hare because he deluded himself by thinking that he could lick his own back.

We want to set an example. The fish has run out of water. Zobohla MaNyosi. It will catch up with him. The tears will flood and dry up, because the sweetness of crime is the bitterness of comeuppance. We want to open a new chapter of justice, and bury prejudice. On the same score, Elephant will also show us where beer is being brewed. (He will face the consequences). He who carries Tortoise on his hand must not cry foul when the confined animal defecates on him. We all know that Elephant played a big role in perpetuating our suffering and humiliation. He stifled our mumblings and jeering's. A torment, he was. Elephant chased away many good birds. Remember, whenever Hare let out bad air that really outraged everyone who was there, Elephant , firstly, did not want to acknowledge that there was an aerial invasion, two, he did not want to see us block our nostrils , and three, he castigated us for complaining that the unpleasant air emanating from his friend and ally was undoubtedly unbearable and unmatched, and lastly he said we should never ever suggest that his dear friend and ally move away or contain it because he would be merely responding to the call of nature! We, however, insisted that if he really cared about and respected other animates, he would know when and how to reign it in next time! " Animals, birds, reptiles and insects could not contain the urge to laugh. Lark's eyes were tearful.

"I remember one day, again, Hare let it off, and it was so pervasive and strong that Ngcethe exclaimed with disgust. Elephant did not take kindly to that exclamation, and ordered the small bird to retract his statement and admit that it was a slip of the tongue on his part. Imagine, he then encouraged us to inhale that poison quietly and blissfully as if our bodies were artificial! It means our well-being was nothing to the two villains. Hare ate things he ate alone by virtue of his greedy heart. He was heartless. He did not give us anything except problems. Now, Elephant wanted us to be passive receivers of Hare's emissions! Oh, please! We all know how Eagle was tortured for saying Hare should behave himself and refrain from letting his tail off his wild aperture now and then in public. Elephant was a menace. He forgot that in the process he was fetching a piece of firewood stuck with a noxious scorpion. Through his actions and words, we can see that he was in effect taking out his own spear and plunging it into his own his body. Yes, step by step, slowly but surely, he was doing more harm to himself than good. Comrades and friends, our illustrious elders said: we don't mourn the culprit, we shed tears for the victim. He who has a bed must lie on it now. In this case, the two cold-blooded criminals will have no choice but to lie on it."

There was a thunderous round of applause. Touchy and sluggish Snail wriggled towards snorting Pig, and for a while, together they seemed to be performing a special duet, a heavenly ritual of conquest with their jiving bodies. That day, Baboon's protruding forehead did not steal the thunder from his vocal dexterity and bodily wizardry. He was singing with a voice of its own life and exhibiting an eye-riveting go-easy dance style he called a get-down sideways. Even the insects and ants shrieked with boundless joy upon hearing that Elephant, who hitherto to gave them a tough time at the beck and call of the hateful Hare would be punished severely.

In fact, chatty Cat clapped his claws, and shouted, "Well done, Snail and Pig! What a scintillating performance to mark a great occasion!" He bent his neck towards Cockroach and remarked, "I am sure we are unanimous that Elephant has to carry his own trunk, because it cannot be too heavy for him now! His mere presence and sight used to get tongues wagging. He was Hare's eyes and ears. He instilled fear in us, we watched whatever we had to say in his presence. Remember, Dog, though loyal as he was-one day decided to say enough is enough. He said it amongst many animals, including Elephant, that he was going to catch Hare with his claws, shake him down to mother earth and bring him to our court, presided over by none other than our respected, tested and dependable elder animals, so that justice could be administered. You know what happened? The following day, Dog disappeared without as much as a howl or trace! It was a common mystery. However, we all know that evil Elephant had a claw in this foul play. And we know too, under whose instructions Elephant was acting. The Day of Justice has been awaiting them. Finally and fortunately, it is here". Cockroach nodded, thinking of how quite Sheep was clubbed by Elephant, acting on the orders of Hare. Elephant had claimed he was beating him up because Sheep had an unsightly habit of keeping mucus on his face. He added that the mucus made him (Elephant) feel like throwing up. However, it turned out that Sheep's crime was his eventual refusal to sing praises for Hare .In a subservient fashion, he used do whatever he was told to do. Hare used to order him to jump and he would ask, "How high, Sir?"

Hare and Elephant were hauled to a court of justice. The ten -member jury had insects, birds, reptiles and animals in it. Bat presided over the deliberations. Every bird, every reptile, every animal and every insect watched the proceedings with keen interest. Hare wanted to talk, but most animals reacted angrily to this. "Shut up, shut up, father of thieves and killers! Your time is up, can't you see? You have no right to address us. After all, we all know that you want to shield yourself with lies! Not this time. Close your big mouth!"Bull-frog, whose neck all along had been vibrating so vividly that partially blind Bat could see, croaked, "You sent Elephant to crush all my children, you evil Hare just because we disagreed on a number of things, especially about your treatment of other animals ,reptiles, insects and birds.

Today, l want to spit on you. Today, you will die between my feet like lice. I will crush you as l spill your blood, bloody sucker!" He was approaching Hare when Bat ordered other animals to hold him back and calm him down. For a while animals seemed to discuss and whisper about the recent actions and words of Bull-frog .Bat cleared his throat and thundered, "Please order! Order! May l call everyone to order .Hush, comrades!" Immediately there was utter silence.

Bat resumed, "Justice is what we seek here?Is that so?"

All the insects, animals, reptiles and birds chorused, "Yes, judge!" Bat pointed at Hare and Elephant, and said, "These animals deserve to see justice in action. Let us not convict them. Let them convict themselves, if need be. Now, l call upon Hare to respond to the accusations that he has been cheating when it comes to running competitions , secondly many birds, animals, reptiles and insects have suffered and perished at his claws." Hare, looking pale and piteous, stood up, and he was atypically shivering. His voice quivered, " Yes, judge. I...l bbb... butchered mmm..more animals, bbb..birds... ree..reptiles, inn....inse cts than l can ...remember.." To think that he used to deliver brilliant and coherent speeches and to compare those presentations to that stuttered revelation was like some kind of a joke or a dream. Animals, reptiles, insects and reptiles were speechless. They were stunned.

Bat asked Elephant to respond to the accusations of perpetuating of an ogre of intimidation's, disappearances and mass murders under the instructions of Hare. He tried to stand up, and as if his trunk was too heavy for him, he flopped on the ground. His mouth was ajar. His breathing was heavy, and before they could do anything the big animal breathed his last. While everyone was trying to come to terms with the fateful tumble of Elephant, Hare collapsed. His body looked motionless and lifeless. Bat ordered Rodent to fetch cold water, wondering whether Hare was not up to his old tricks. Cold water was poured over the body of the speedy animal. However, cold water did not resurrect Hare from the dead. He was cold...

Meanwhile, Cat could not believe that Hare was dead. His mind wondered to the fact that was no secret, the truth that he had killed and eaten many an animal by playing a cooking game with them. They said he was worse than a hen that ate her own eggs, and then professed ignorance of their stealthy decrease and disappearance.

Though he was advanced in age, toothless and hard of hearing, he relished tucking into other animal's meat. He derived pleasure from eating game. And he always had a game up his sleeve. The soot of his pot he always ingeniously rubbed it off on other animals. The game usually started like this: Hare would ask the other animals to heave him up into a huge pot under which a fire raged. A lid would be slapped on the three legged vessel. When the inside of the container got too searing to bear, he would ask the other beast to take out the lid and promptly take him out. Telling the other animal to relax, he would help it to climb up into the pot and slam the lid on with a cynical smile.

However, after a while when the other animal duly requested to be rescued from the high temperature, he merrily sang, "Burn my little animal, burn!" The other animal would probably plead, "Please, please open up the pot. I'm being fried alive!" He would sing with contentment," Yes, that suits you well, my little animal! Tshana nyamazana yami tshana(Burn my little animal, burn!)" . The poor animal would thus be clandestinely cooked and eaten by none other than him.

He and only he would enjoy the meat like a glutton and after the meal, whistle through the bone opening of that animal, boasting," I said let us cook one another, he agreed. But l ended up cooking him!" Sometimes he would trick a creature and leave him holding on to a boulder! He considered other clawed animals' meat as his favourite relish.

Cat was still thinking of the antics and travesties of justice committed by Hare and his crony when Bat asked everyone to help ferry the two bodies to a nearby anthill where the deceased would be laid to rest. Ants, birds, animals and reptiles did not shirk the task at hand. They struggled with the bodies, panting, falling and picking themselves up until they arrived at the final resting place for the two friends, and foes of everyone. The anthill was a hub for termites.

After the burial, Tortoise became the animal of the moment, the centre of attraction. He climbed over a tree and addressed the swelling crowd. He looked humble and calm. Even his usually hard and rocky body looked shiny and squashy. The horde of animals and birds thundered, "Tortoise! Tortoise! Be our servant leader!" He took a long breath. His greeting words were greeted with thunderous ovation. He mentioned that animals came in many and various forms, sizes and shapes, and that it was common to lump them together for different reasons. He also stressed that animals usually worked as a team to gather food in an effective and efficient way, for grooming, for protection, for raising of their young, for migration and of course, life was too short to be spent whining about- for playing as well. In response to this laughter and whistles shot up. Though he suffered bouts of stammering and characteristic sluggishness, monotony did not see the light of the day as every animal and bird was all ears.

"Just like our bleating or chirping, we all seek to live and thrive. We seek abundant lives. We are animals. We are mammals. The bottom line is that we're all animates. Whether clawed animal or not. Whether reptile or not. Whether bird or insect. Whether black or white. Whether big or small. Whether smelly or smart. What's the point of laughing narcissistically at the physical appearance of one animal? Suppose you're Baboon then you start to say Hippo's ugliness is suffocating. OK...Fine for you for a while. Think deeper. Now, if Hippopotamus says, well, enough is enough, and hurls the live snake at you, and says Baboon your protruding forehead is just too sharp-edged for comfort.

In fact, it's like a spear! It makes us jittery. We don't want to live jumpy lives forever. What happens? Anxieties take centre stage. The stage is set for tension to mount, for tempers flare up. What ensures? A war of words that can turn nasty. And you claim to be smart? How can you be so ambivalent as to be nasty and smart? Hate and love at the same time? An author of confusion and destruction. No. A vicious cycle of bickering, breaking, bragging and even biting does not make this forest a better place to live in. It makes it bitter rather than better. It makes it hellish and devilish. We don't need such a habitat. We don't need devils in our midst. We don't need confusionists running loose. Neither do we need destroyers disguised as builders and peace-makers.

"What happens to Giraffe also happens to Lion. Laugh at an invalid when you are no more . Beyond the grave. That's what our foresighted elders admonished us to bear in mind. Do not ever laugh at the wound of another animate. For you don't know whether tomorrow your body will remain intact and healthy. We know that it is not encouraged for someone to talk ill of the dead, but let us face it. This is the moment of truth. Hare did not laugh with other animals, instead he smiled at them, and how? In his insincere and insidious ways, he smiled at them. He is infamous. He authoured other animals' miseries. History has it. It is recorded. His misdeeds. As if that were not enough, he gloated over their wretchedness, he presided over their ruins, and their sense of helplessness whilst his wife whistled and giggled, curled up in an expansive grasscushioned couch. Such was Hare. Hare, who is lying there. His actions were divisive and sinister. He favoured those who did not question things or who clapped claws or feet or wings for him, no matter how lost he was. He hated with a passion those who sought to correct his wrongs. Destruction he fed them. Destruction was his trump-card. That is his legacy. During times of our misfortunes, for example, long dry spells and drought, what did he do? He shed gallons and gallons of precious but crocodile tears through his cynical tirades and eulogies. What a shameless pretender, he was. Never genuine and remorseful. He was ever manipulative, brutal and slippery. He was one of the meanest animals to live under his self-imposed rule. A reign of terror. "Bull –frog bellowed, "He is in Hell now!"

Nonetheless Tortoise continued with his speech, "This is a dawn of love and unity, a sunrise of hope and humility, a time to forge ahead. This is not my task alone. It is too heavy for one animate to carry alone. l risk breaking down if you don't come to the party. Carry your cross. I carry my cross. This is our struggle. Our collective duty and responsibility. Our exercise for the restoration of dignity and freedom. Our regeneration . Our rebirth. Lessons of the past have been learnt. We can't be seen receding, yes eating the vomit of the times of yore. The era of Hare and his sooty ways is over. He made us look dirty and always used us as his scapegoat. He was mired in mess and callousness but was in mulish denial. Damage and decay are his legacy. If one day someone had said: Hare has suffered a heart attack. Would we have accepted or believed the news? No ways! A big NO. We couldn't have. Why? ***He couldn't suffer a heart attack because he had no heart***. He was heartless. However, the past events should inform us, teach us, guide us and arm us with the map to chart out the way forward.

We are our liberators through our actions and visions".

There was another round of applause. The rains soaked the soil of the bush like never before. What a hauntingly rare day it turned out to be.

A Speechless Assault Crime Story And Other Little Stories

My eyes fell upon a tattered, old and abandoned copy of the much-loved Mahlabezulu community newspaper. It was frighteningly greasy and messy as if it had been used as toilet paper once or twice before but l could not resist the urge to pick it up. Possibly the greasiness and messiness of the paper wheedled me into action. I read about a couple that was arrested for not only brutalizing their children, but also for marrying off two of their teenage daughters to two hairless and toothless octogenarians respectively in exchange of beer and two tiny goats. My face twitched into a dreadful frown.

I paused and momentarily my mind meandered away, away to a bizarre story that was narrated by my friend, Rhodes a few years back...

"The twenty-something year old man secretly entered a woman's house. It was at night and the lady was sleeping under her mosquito net in her bedroom".

The narrator had paused for some time, laughter getting the better of him. "What happened?"

I had asked curiously, impatience saying: let us go mate. Rhodes—the narrator, my colleague and friend —had told me countless crazy stories. Not this one. This one was something else.

"The lady woke up only to discover that there was a man lying on top of her. Not only was he on top of her, he was also trying to take off her clothes. Can you guess what happened next?"

I had thought that was an easy question. "She screamed at the top of her voice". That had been my prompt and confident response. I had responded with confidence and eagerness. However, according to Rhodes, the story had its twists and turns.

"Actually, on discovering that the lady was astir, the stranger decided to be a bit romantic by kissing her, and the woman did not disappoint because she quickly opened her mouth wide as the man buried his tongue into it. Then...she bit his tongue so hard that it was cut off and remained in her mouth!

The stunned man fled for dear life, BLEEDING. However, the pain was so unbearable that soon he sought medical attention at a local hospital. He was arrested for his sexual assault crime."

I remembered how a series of wows reeled out of my mouth. It floored me. Rhodes had said he found the commentators' analysis more intriguing than the story itself. "Some people claimed he would use sign language to warn other rapists that crime does not pay at all. Other people teased that he would kiss goodbye to expressions like: I'm tongue- tied or tongue in cheek. One guy imagined if the investigators asked the felon what happened, he would probably confess: I'm speechless".

The next page had its other half cut off. On what was left of that page l read about a self-confessed prophet, miraclespinner and pastor whom the congregants bowed down to, and whatever he decreed he was granted without any modicum of hesitation and questioning by his vulnerable church members, including claiming members' cars, credit cards and twenty percent of their monthly income, and of course capping his supremacy with a little spice of gallivanting with his chosen men, teenage girls and married women on dubious holy crusades. Seething anger seemed to choke my heart and so my eyes momentarily leapt to another page.

The sub-heading was: Miracle Ebony And Ivory Quadruplet. There was a picture of a young, beautiful black religious sister who had given birth to four healthy female miracle babbling babies .On one side there was one pair of little pitch-dark girls. They were like charcoal in colour and beauty in vividness. On the other side, were two little lovely white babies. The pictures of the four children seemed to breathe and depict a certain living innocence. All of the babies had dark curly hair that coaxed one to brush it with one's fingers, or so the journalist wrote. At the bottom, l took a cursory look at the readers' comments and responses, and my eyes landed on a phrase, "White as snow, our sins should be transformed…"Without getting the gist of the statement l immediately skipped that section.

The opinion page carried an article that breathed fire and vomited verbal volcano. It was curiously titled Of Daylight Thieves, Stinking Salaries and Sinking Economy. In his introduction the columnist stated without any tinge of regret that he once pummeled a chief executive officer into submission and "transitory coma" at an upmarket cocktail bar after he had told him, (the columnist) that he was a mere "tiny peanuts boy" who should not have been frequenting that exclusive palatial bar "normally and befittingly" graced by highly paid bigwigs, members of parliament, ministers, company directors, respected board members, parastatal and municipal bosses and their queenly wives and mistresses. In the body of his critique he disclosed that he had lost hope and confidence in the arms of government to serve the citizens with impartiality, citing many cases of injustice that had left him shell-shocked and disgruntled.

The skeptic also bemoaned a chronic lack of capacity on the part of government to discharge key functions and responsibilities, adding that there was a bad and tired leadership on one side, and abundant resources on the other. He attacked government for adopting an embarrassing multicurrency system, a development which clearly showed their pseudo-Pan-Africanism because all the five currencies which were being formally accepted for use were not from a single African country. He also lambasted parastatal bosses whose ridiculously astronomical salaries were gobbling up state funds, saying a lack of transparency, audited reports and corporate governance was a cause for concern. The writer and activist said the irony of it was that against the backdrop of non-performance, bankruptcy, obsolete infrastructure, the liquidity crunch, a poor remuneration and exploitation of junior employees and an unrelenting drop in the quality of service delivery, yet the parastatal and municipal bosses continued to award themselves disproportionately high salaries.

He concluded that this combination translated into a startlingly stubborn nightmare for the nation, and hence called upon unions and citizens with a shred of conscience to march into all the state enterprises and local authorities managed by those greedy bosses and demand their immediate sucking, and the freezing of their financial assets pending non-partisan and thorough investigations and publication of the findings. Claiming that the state coffers were bleeding, he wrote that the time of pampering the poisonous burdens and obscenities of dictatorship, of sugar-coating shit, of cuddling corrupt individuals and cronies was over. Mass action was going to sweep off all the rot

.Citizens had to take back what was stolen from them by all means possible. Those who took the citizens' resilience, understanding and patience for granted were courting real trouble and its grandparents. His final sentence was: The gnashing of teeth is imminent. I was thinking of the over-zealousness of the officers in relation to the possible vicarious liability of their seniors in that incident and other acts.

Maybe the situation was such that if one did not seek the favour of man by running to the opposite extreme, then hunger was what one would put on the family table? Did the elders not conclude that hunger coerces people to tuck into their filth? Was the mere act of seeking to please man not a snare and a sign of slavery? Just like school incidents which often reflect children's attitudes at home, the influence of the officers' self-conceited superiors was loud and visible. Incidents of prejudice and politics children exhibit in society or at school, to a certain extent, are a reflection of what they pick up from the actions and words of their parents or guardians. If young children discriminate against other different social groups, the buck stops at the door of the parents and guardians. Dealing with the young students, at that stage, could be tantamount to attacking a mere symptom. After all, officers were carrying out their duties under instructions, and perhaps to shoot the messenger is to misfire.

Thinking of students sent my childhood memories flooding into my head, as I thought of such games as Statue, Man and Wife and other Simulations, Hide and Seek, Puzzles, Look(someone would tease one and exclaim at a funny object, for example a cockroach, yet in reality there was none),Your Mother's Breasts(in the bushes bullies pushed "their subjects" into literally herding cattle on their behalf and into imprudent fist fights by drawing someone else's mother's breasts on the ground , and suggesting that one herder erase the sketch . Then they would ask the other boy whether he was happy with the fact that the diagram of his mother's breasts was rubbed out. If he said he were unhappy they would say, "This is all bark but no bite, show him that you have love and respect for your mother and discipline him for his act of disrespect for her". More often than not fierce fighting ensured. I also played Ntsoro,(the cumulative throwing of little stones into little burrows on the ground) , R,(the skipping into designated drawn patterns on the ground at some points using one leg),and , the all-day plastic ball matches were even better than the Snake Ladder competitions at night. Father did not allow card playing at home or elsewhere because he thought it encouraged gambling tendencies, and the stealing of money and idleness, and hence l never got to understand and know how people juggled with them. My cousins and their friends secretly played and squirreled them away before he could arrive from work. I saw street fejafejas (the pavement gamblers who rip off the gullible passers-by). I heard of shattered marriages, souring or severed relationships, of families sleeping on empty stomachs courtesy of street gambling. Maybe it was not a good idea, l thought.

I think l was, on average, an obedient, likable boy who listened and tried to follow instructions from elders. There are certain prohibitions or clan taboos that have to be observed by members of particular clans. Certain animals were associated with one's clan, and no matter how one loved tucking into meat, they would not dare eat the flesh of the animal representing their family name. For example, the Khumalos would not eat fish, the Ncubes respected the baboon, the Dubes held the zebra in high esteem, while the Ndlovus' totem animal was the elephant. They even warned that those who ate meat of their totem animals had no- one else to blame if their teeth prematurely fell off or decayed because of such acts of insolence. The treatment and the disposal of the umbilical cord and the placenta are crucial as different clans have different ways of performing this proclamation rite. However, the end result is to bring a sense of belonging and security to the newly born child.

There was a story that once did rounds in my village. It was said that a beautiful young woman was married to one Khumalo man who worked in Jozi (Johannesburg), and only came home once or twice per year. In November the loving wife was alleged to have sent urgent petitions after petitions to her husband to come back home, as she was missing him so much that it hurt after a year of his absence. The couple had one child. Come December, the injiva(people who worked in South Africa, were given that reference when they came back home on a visit) heaved in sight amid jubilation from his family and relatives. After Christmas, the miner went back to one of his gold mines down South. He joined the characteristic great trek. The man's ego was on a high note a few days later when his young wife wrote him a thank you letter for "leaving behind his stamp". In the letter his wife told him that she was having sporadic bouts of vomiting. The miner read between the lines. He was so excited that he shared with a number of his workmates the good news from his loving wife. "Last year but one I did it. We're a few days into the New Year, and already l have a new gift! l leave my signature each time l go home. A man has to feed his family. Leave them satisfied. My wife's stomach is now full! I fed her with the right quantity and quality of food", he boasted.

* * *

After nine months, the much-awaited baby was born. Upon the fall of the umbilical cord, an old woman took it to the river. She carefully and slowly chipped the dry cord stub on a rock in the river. As the clan's way of offering the baby to the ancestors, she pleaded for protection and abundance. She expected the swimming fish to at least pick up the pieces. To her amazement, the fish seemed not to notice the presence of the pieces in the water. If anything, they just swam away from them! She waited and waited, but the fish just ignored the pieces. As she went home, she was wearing a lugubrious and wondering expression. Did it mean the young lady had been unfaithful? Why did the ancestors reject the chips? Why would they reject their own child? Why would they rebuff their own blood? Months later, when the child cried like a real cry baby, pestering the mother in the hut or in the fields or at the river well , she would go out , away from everyone else, and say something to her little one, and the child would suddenly stop sobbing! People believed she called out the surname and praise names of the reserved man who herded the family's cattle and goats.

I learnt about the origins of the totems and their relationships with the different clans from an elder. There was a need for families to have an authoritative head after the demise of the communities' nomadic life. Living in their fortresses of caves, the communities needed some distinguishing mechanism as they sought better protection from other more powerful, harassing and cantankerous groups. The adoption of totems became a distinguishing feature. The animal that was adopted did not only become a patron but also a spiritual member of the group which commanded respect and sacredness.

I also remembered the Ndebele mythology of the hair-raising human-like creatures that were believed to inhabit the dense forests. The amazimu were said to have protruding cheek bones, jutted teeth, claws on their fingers and strong unsightly bodies that enabled them to catch their victims and as cannibals gnaw a bone and guzzle it within a matter of seconds. In the yarns spun by grandmothers and grandfathers, it was said travelers fell victim to these bush terrors, and in their witty way, they would allure girls, keep and feed them in their hideouts, and eat them up when they had gained weight. Sometimes, the thickness of the forest gave me a fright, though on my few visits to the rural areas l had a yearning to explore nature through the thick bushes.

I feared going near a pool or dam whose water did run dry year in and year out because people claimed such places were prone to be havens for mermaids. I thought of our oral traditions, our morals and our heritage, especially the legends featuring tender rocks and stones, animals speaking with other animates, for example, the fable of Unwabu, the chameleon who was sent by the Creator to advise people that they would not perish. However, Untulo, the lizard overheard the message and hijacked it by tearing away with amazing speed to the people and to misinform them that they would die. It was no surprise that when Unwabu delivered the message from the Creator people squarely told him that they would not buy his story because Untulo had told them a diametrically different one. According to that legend as a result of Untulo's twisted message the people died. That was the Creation Story from the Ndebele traditional perspective. It spoke to the young about wisdom, exemplary demeanor and the vagaries of life.

Belief and culture are one side of the same coin. I was taught about the significance of some beliefs and signs by my father's eldest brother. My eldest uncle told me that he had warts on his arms and legs when young. Culturally, that was a sign that he would have boys. However, he wanted to have girls (possibly he wanted to have as many cattle as possible from suitors!), and so he ran a broom over them. This was a way of saying: boys stop, girls here you come! That was not to be. It looked like the boys were unfazed and deaf to the rejection. They came anyway! I asked him whether he doubted the accuracy of such predictions and signs, but he gave me another picture about his life.

He told me that he was six years when the falling out of the milk-set of his teeth began. As the community believed that that this stage of development meant that umzwazwa(black kite) would see it fit to procure his new teeth in order to replace the lost ones, he was happy and expectant. "Mzwazwa, collect this tooth of mine. It's bad and l don't want it any more. Please, give me yours, I know it's good. "He described for me how he confidently took one of his teeth and mumbled a spell, after which he bent down and threw away the tooth towards the bird, in a backward fashion, through his legs. I remembered asking him about the result of this ritual. His response was rather solemn: I don't think umzwazwa heard me at all. If that bird were here, I would tell it to bring back my original teeth unconditionally so I could eat meat like some of my age mates!

WHY STANDTOLL AND TRYMORE COLLAPSED

It was their humble version of *The Country Has Talent*. Guess who stood up as the judge readied to unveil the winners? Your guess is as good as mine... Standtoll was set upright, so was Trymore. Both claimed to be victors. What a standoff! Was there a draw? People were curious. The judge was serious.

When the arbiter talked about the penultimate contestant, Standtoll, thought of himself as the best.

Trymore tried to tell Standtoll that he was the winner! He was telling everybody to congratulate him.

Both contestants were coy about their ages, the judge disclosed. Said the stout official "Standtoll, you're the penultimate contender". Standtoll hopped up and down with joy. She added, "It means you're next to Trymore, the very last guy!"

Friendly Wars

Ever since his appointment to the lofty position of defense minister, he seemed to be gripped by some phobia. Some residents claimed the irrational fear stemmed from the possibility that he did not know what he was expected to do. Others thought that he was a lucky coward who found himself having to oversee a strategic security portfolio which he did not deserve or understand.

Mr. Gubuzela's political history was not well-known in the country except for the controversial claims he made each time he had an opportunity about his heroic past during the liberation war. Not only were the citizens unconvinced about his war liberation credentials , they were also skeptical of his ability to turn around the national army into a truly professional , patriotic and non-partisan force that could be the envy of the region, if not the continent . It had committed untold atrocities in the country and beyond national boundaries.

He was once labeled a "Wild Useless Claimant" by a nononsense newspaper when he claimed that all the country's political and economic woes were visited upon the nation by the "stubborn" opposition leaders, the ruling party's detractors and their Western allies.

What was a known fact was that he was a shameless bootlicker who heaped praises upon the ruining leadership with sickening frequency and subservience. It was no secret that he was a Grade Two primary school dropout who had endeared himself to the leadership by worshiping them at every rally or meeting , and terrorizing any soul who challenged the big wig's bigotry and destructive policies at every conceivable corner. He would declare," Some of us died for this country. We won't allow any person, especially from the opposition to rule this country. These sellouts without liberation war credentials are day-dreamers. Forward with our one and only revolutionary leader. Down with all the detractors! Down with illegal sanctions!"

There Is A Method In Her Madness

"Does this bring food to my little table? How many times should I tell villagers here that I no longer want to hear about that name? Do you want my granddaughters and sons who are sweating it out in foreign lands to starve me after getting wind that I am attending useless meetings arranged by the same crazy and clueless fellows who ran everything down and as if that were not enough damage— chased good citizens through violence and hunger? Look at you: unemployed, starving and coming here with: Gogo, there's a meeting. What! Wake up. You want me to vomit? Get out, out!!!" Granny Masuku's stick landed hard and severally on an image emblazoned on the front of the visitor's worn-out shirt.

The visitor was sent packing. For the first time, he asked himself whether over the years he had really benefited from organizing and terrorizing people or whether he was just being used by the big greedy officials. He felt naked, foolish and embarrassed.

That incident sent the village wagging tongues. Some people said it was because of senility or madness or both. All agreed that whatever it was there was a mantra and a method in it.

Gogo: SiNdebele for grandmother

Something Gnaws

Nkululeko Ndlela smiled, exposing his even teeth that were yellowish from neglect and tireless pulls of begged cigarettes. He was marveling at the scantily dressed youthful female dancers who seemed to regale the crowd not only with their striking voices and footwork, but also with their lacy tighties that vividly outlined all the contours of their gyrating bodies.

Nkululeko wondered: could this be a sizzling rhumba show?

But no as I entered this building I clearly saw this acronymHHA. Could these young women, who obviously lower the moral standard of this place, be members of the Holy and Heavenly Saints of Afrika? Hmmm anyway, I don't care a whit about what place and who the heck ... as long as I get what I die for, that's fine ....

There was a sizable crowd in the building, with a coterie of the well-dressed people, mainly the aged and wrinkled, seated on a raised area facing the rest on the benches. The exclusive group of the octogenarians and centenarians were ensconced in raised gold and silver arm chairs, belching, soliloquizing, dozing off and frothing forth on the mouth. At the entrance, people of all ages trickled in, but the white haired dodderers balancing on their walking sticks seemed to outnumber the young folk.

Two young souls, Thembi and Sihle sat on the bench as intimate to each as the copulating turtle doves. Sihle keeled her giraffe-like neck over the broad shoulders of her lover and remarked, "Hope keeps us from throwing in the towel. But, don't you think one of these days one would end up throwing up? Really, can one stand …." She was stopped in her tracks by the almost spontaneous crescendo of chanting and dancing, emanating from the VIP group in the front, sporadically cascading to the audience at all the flanks of the building.

However, Nkululeko's mind was drifting off. Yesterday, it was. Yes, I drifted into a crowd at Vevane Beit Hall. I can picture it all, their determination, their voices, I can hear even. The oratorical skills of that short ad sharp dread-locked man who made an impassioned plea. His booming voice still resonates in my ears. Did he not say, "What has come over us? The poor are getting poorer and poorer by the day while the haves tart up their citadel of failures and follies. The chasm between the haves and have-nots is yawning. The have nots lead a lie if they are told that they have and accept. Were we not cut out for better things? We were not liberated so that we can enjoy the fruits of independence? Where are those fruits? We have an abundance of mineral resources, but is the country benefiting? We now live a lie and we know it. We accept it. That's worse. We are cursed with our own follies and failings.

Cut throats, we bestow honour after honour. We stoop low of our own volition. Why? Don't cut throats make our flesh creep and society unsafe? Their blood curdling acts, we gladly sugarcoat as virtues and valour. When our rights are taken away, the best we can do is smile rather than snarl. So good as to be bad pawns, we are like fawns, we fall over each other trying to win the affection of the cut throats.

Grouching worshipfully to them, and even licking their feet, their bums. Dirty! What flagrant profanity! Impurity foists all sewage on us. And we resign into it. Where are the good men and women? Let the good men and women be counted. Good men and women, be the deliverers in the face of adversity. Something gnaws at my conscience. That's why I have to stand up ...

He was jolted into reality by the sudden raising of the people from the back flattening benches and frantic whistling, thunderous hand clapping and chanting from the VIP section. There was a bustle and hustle as the cameras snapped and flashed with fury. The VIP burst into another song and dance. Nkululeko's eyes were searching for the black man of the cloth from the States. He was reported to be 75 years and as having a long beard. He was also reported to be a welltraveled performer of miracles. Nkululeko wondered whether there was something for him or he had wondered whether there was something for him or he had wandered off into the wrong place. He started to believe that he would dart out of that place a satisfied man. He was confident at the end of the day he would claim to be better than those who twiddle their thumps or grumble themselves hoarse at home.

The men in the twilight of their lives were literally falling over each other to shake hands with that arrival, whose head, by any definition and standard competed with the hippo's for honours in the world of unsightliness. A child did not need to be a cry-baby to have a series of nightmares and nocturnal cries after catching sight of that bulky man. Where others had dimples he had wrinkles, when others breathed he snorted like a pig. Indeed, the presence of that solidly built man attracted and held the attention of Nkululeko like lamp to moth. What went for the hair were a few grains that grew in isolated tufts. From that point of view, he looked every centimeter an oddity and monstrosity. In the eyes of Nkululeko looking at him could just get one driver's mind's at a road junction in a tumult.

Several groups and individuals went upstage to perform some dances, croon some melodies or recite some praise poems. In a flash, the whole congregation had their eyes riveted to a troupe of women in white robes who sang, danced and ducked in a fantastically ritualistic fashion. Nkululeko was thinking. These agile, religious women are hotting up the pulpit for that visiting American clergyman. He must be a type of glutton to be that stout, surely. People shall eat out of his stumpy hands. Where is the long beard? Anyway, that is insignificant, as long as I .... In the twinkle of an eye, a lanky man in tattered overalls, in the tradition and mould of a clown or a wag, galloped towards the VIP section and in slow motion squatted in front of the stout man clad in an immaculate white suit. The waggish man squawked with his head and hands raised skyward in a prayerful and worshipful poise.. "Humble chef, murihombe(you are huge). But my stomach rumbles because ...." Some powerful men pounced upon him, probably impugning his motives. As the man was being dragged kicking and screaming, Nkululeko was thinking. Perhaps that man is mad or was impetuous to expect the African-American to exorcise him before the delivery of his sermon. Or did the cyclic dancing of the women in white robes galvinise him into a trance?

However, Nkululeko overheard the cross- legged Sihle comment, "He is neither mad nor uneducated. He has children and a wife to render guardianship of but the national centre can no longer hold. That fat arrival is having the time of his life with a certain grass widow whose husband is in the Diaspora." Nkululeko could not believe what he was hearing! The muchtalked about miracle spinning pastor was mired in infidelity. But no! People were casting aspersions and accusations at him for he had just arrived in the country. Sihle continued, "Thembi,

I wonder what charges are going to be preferred upon that poor soul who invaded the VIP section? Hope no sandpaper and electricity will be applied to his private parts. I am not grumpy or unpatriotic but when is a stop going to be put to the arbitrary arrests on an array of often spurious charges based on some sections of a draconian? "She halted as fear coursed down her spine by virtue of a dandy in dark glasses who heaved in sight. The couple exchanged knowing glances while the smartly dressed man went past them.

The bulky man who was the centre of attention finally stood up. This was coupled with a roar of applause from the VIP section. He paused and smiled, and Nkululeko cold see the flesh on his cheeks gather in clumsy folds. His voice was stentorian, but to Nkululeko's amazement, he spoke with a heavy accent in vernacular! This prompted Nkululeko to ask Thembi, "In what capacity is this man addressing the audience?" Thembi replied, "He is a minister." Nkululeko rapped out, "A church minister from the States you mean?" It was Sihle's time to quip, and quip she did effortlessly. "C'mon, brother... Is this rapacious bumble-bee from the USA? Good gracious! He is a high ranking political minister. Wait until he starts political posturing and this place will go off the rails!"

Nkululeko did not despair. He was curious to find out why Thembi and Sihle were there. "Risking being viewed as too intrusive, would you be comfortable to fill me in on your mission here? Are you members of the Holy and Heavenly Saints of Afrika or members of a political party this minister is also affiliated with? Sorry to sound like a nosy newshawk, but ...." Thembi chipped in, "Brother, you don't have to be apologetic. If a thing stinks, well it stinks, full stop. If a ship sinks, he thinks we should not say: it sinks! But the truth is that: any failure of this magnitude stinks. No amount of suppression or lying will save the ship from sinking. Yet this boils down to the basics of politics: shape up or ship out, if you can't stand the heat, get the heck out of the kitchen. I don't have to mince my words while I am suffocating. Oh ...to answer question: no, we are not the Holy and Heavenly Saints of Afrika, the holier-than-thou fanatics who accept at sacrificing the poor on the altar of political expediency." He took a long thoughtful pause before saying, "We are political science students working on our research projects. My research problem deals with the authenticity of the election results in Matsheni as indicators of the popularity of the ru ..." Sihle gave her lover a little pat on his right shoulder." Sweetheart, the political gasbag is at. Listen to his gospel. The gospel according to ..." Her boyfriend cut her off with a suppressed laugh." Oh, please stop there!" The minister was greeting all the colossi in the VIP section and all and sundry on the premises. He heaped praises upon his political party, the party officials and supporters and said it was the best thing that had ever happened to the nation of Matsheni. Sihle could only gasp, "NX! What drivel!" Thembi said, "Now heed his advice, he seems to be addressing us." The veteran politician was saying, "The youth lack civility, self-control and a sense of belonging. They go along with the destructive winds into cultural and political wilderness that are surmountable challenges like shortages of food, water, fuel, accommodation, transport and foreign currency. The hypocritical Western countries are in complicit. The suffering is visited upon the nation by senseless detractors and their sponsors. We try to explain basic things to them as repositories of wisdom and role models, but they show no respect for the elders."

There was a collection of whitish foam on the edges of his mouth. Sihle stood up before whispering to Thembi, "Tshomi(friend), let me visit the ladies' while you listen to him rant and rave. But to say all the elders are the repositories of wisdom or good role models is to hold on to an obvious delusion to put it mildly. Integrity, guys. Talk of the old hands in Matsheni's cookie jar!" She weaved her way towards to word: Exit on the wall.

Nkululeko inquired, "Mpintshi(friend), what could have happened to the African American who was expected to deliver a sermon here?" Thembi tilted her neck towards Nkululeko. He calmly relied, "A foreign TV station reported that he was arrested shortly after arriving in Matsheni after preaching on a street that people should not worry about the acute shortage of food because in Heaven they shall not hunger. You wanted to hear him preach, tshomi?"

Nkululeko cleared his throat. "I am very hungry and desperate. I am not a Christian, neither I am trying to get him to convert me into one. I drift in search of food. One day I got myself into a procession, and guess what. It turned out to be no food procession but a cortege. Deprivation stalks the land. The other day, I bumped into a group of men and women who were running. I joined in the race secure in the belief that they were heading for a shop where bags of mealie-meal were being sold. I was alarmed to be warned, all of a sudden to duck and dodge because the knife-wielding pickpocket had U-turned and was coming at me! I leapt to my left in a straight-from a- moviescript fashion, bantu!(people). In these fuel and food queues, it is common for tempers to flare up and sometimes it can be so tumultuous that fatal fights are inevitable. We live in a society characterized by shortages of water, fuel, accommodation, transport, foreign currency and electricity. Running around in search of food is the order of the day."

Sihle was back. She looked excited," Guys, I used to think that people were bent on tarnishing the H.H.S officials, saying their church was built with party money...Well, it seems there is something sinister here. Do you know that I have just discovered that bags of mealie-meal and sugar are being sold here, and the clandestine dealers are realizing astronomical sums of money? This building is cesspit of corruption and prostitution. It is cesspool of money laundering, profiteering and hard drug trafficking. Residential stands and farms are being sold upstairs as we talk." Disgust gripped Themba and Nkululeko. Nkululeko's body seemed to transform internally. He could feel it. It was both physical and spiritual. The heart that was beating inside him was a stout one. The spirit that had descended upon him was awesome. The fat man paused and regarded his audience before declaring.

"It is my singular honour and privilege to unveil your future mayor. Vote for him. He was cut out for a mayoral office because of his maturity, vision, exemplary liberation war credentials and highest sense of patriotism. He is 99 years old.

Please, stand up, you worship ..." An old bespectacled myopic man, possibly cursed with a backache and other numerous ailments, delicately balancing on a colourful walking stick ,tottered towards the audience. He walked with an unsteady stoop as if he would pick-up something and before he could raise his hands in the air to greet the crowd, he tumbled on the platform like a watermelon.

Meanwhile, Nkululeko's head was struggling with a whirlwind of echoing words: Let the good men and women be counted. That's why I have to stand up. If Nkululeko stood up, no-one ever thought he was girding up his loins. In a trice, he stood up and thundered. "No-oo! This is our posterity you are trifling with. Look at the time piece! We want food! Food!" All hell broke loose as all the young people chorused

"Food!". Some of the toothless elders concurred and swished, "Yeshee! Food! We are tired of cheering people who starve ashee". Then the booing took centre stage. Terrified, the bulky minister took to his heels and hopped into his car, before it cruised away. With sublime indifference Nkululeko led the chorusing group towards the VIP section and some of the old folk came a cropper without as much as receiving a mere push. There was pandemonium as some officers tried to manacle Nkululeko. The young people would not let their ringleader become an early picking. They outflanked and outdone their enemies. As they trooped out of the building, Sihle started a revolutionary song with amazing conviction and with a force of its own life....

On the streets, people in food, fuel, housing and transport queues, abandoned their snaking lines and joined Nkululeko's group. Women and student organizations were in the fold as well. At Gcwalamuzi Shopping Complex, Nkululeko addressed the crowd that had swelled into several millions. He could not believe that he was addressing such a multitude. He spoke about a galloping inflation, alarming levels of corruption, looting of mineral resources, robberies and essential items being sold hugger-mugger, astronomical college fees, low student pay-outs, harassment of the poor and vulnerable and chronic shortage of food and fuel coupled with the promulgation of oppressive laws and the gagging of newspapers and human rightists. Sihle condemned the subversion of democratic electoral processes, abuse of women and children, politics of hate and callousness and populist policies of imprudence and callousness. An old man bemoaned the lack of men of integrity and vision who would be the stool-pigeons in the face of a series of shortages. The crowd was in unison. The powerful, the influential the connected and police would be nabbed! No to sweeping corruption under the carpet! Proposals were made on the way forward. Strategies were mapped out.

Word spread like wildfire. Crowds mushroomed on each and every street. Traffic came to a halt. Shops began to close. Industrial workers downed their tools. There was hurly-burly, hubbub and hullabaloo as the crowds fought running battles with opposing forces. As Nkululeko led his charges of goodwill towards the industrial site the police waylaid them. They were happy with their piece of stratagem put in place to crush the unlawful day-dreaming drifters. But bravado prevailed over barricades! It seemed everyone had hurled away the sissy-like heart and replaced it with a stout one. They had come out of their former docile bodies. Even if it once erected the highest mountain on their way, they seemed to have the resolve to climb or push it aside!

It was astounding. One woman who was a vendor asked? "Shamarwi„ what does Nkululeko mean?"The young handsome journalist who had once been detained for uncovering an electoral fraud replied, 'Take on board freedom! Welcome aboard. It means freedom, mama." She inquired again,"What about Sihle?" The scribe smiled, "It stands for something good." The woman was grateful. "Mwana wangu, one more question, what about Thembi?" The award-winning reporter had a twinkle in the eye. "Thembi is about hope." The woman then shouted with all the force she could summon up, "Freedom is hope because both are good!" However, the crowd made a rendition of the song, and sang, "It is good to have hope because it begets freedom." That piece soon transformed into some kind of a national anthem on the streets for the protesters.

Zibusise Ndlela was jarred out of sleep at 5.35am on the pavement of Kudla Shop. He yawned, realizing he had been in the mealie-meal queens since midnight. Melusi Moyo, another war vet asked, "Comrade, why were you shouting Nkululeko! Nkululeko! At night?" Ndlela spoke in disarmingly candid detail, "You know that my name means Independence. My son at college is Nkululeko. I have always slammed him for being peevish and disobedient at college, demonstrating over the hiking of fees and the like. But comrade, that dream was a revelation. I can confess that I am undergoing a major spiritual and ideological metamorphosis. It taught me as an elder to run my nose over my armpit, lest the odour emanates from me. I was omnipresent, seeing and hearing everything."

He felt biting morning cold air and repeated, "Comrade, something gnaws at my conscience ..."

Then one day one foreign journalist decided to ask him one general question. "Sir, please shed light on what you are doing or intend doing as minister of defense to keep soldiers fit?"

He was clad in his civilian clothes in the form of dazzling yellow socks, white shoes, a red pair of baggy trousers, a green T-shirt, and a dark and blue, deeply cupped hat that seemed to bury his head and obstruct his view of the world. With exaggerated steadiness, he cleared his throat and said, "Soon l will start some friendly wars with neighboring countries".

THE PAIR IS BEYOND REPAIR

The morning is cold and windy. He wobbles on the side of the road while time and again an emergency taxi rattles past him after making pestering and persistent tootles. As an ET clanks on what used to be a tarred road- the dust so twirled off -assails him and he coughs and spits on the ground, cursing rather loudly. "Bullshit. This life we live here. Hell! Bullshit ...Shit."

"Baba Hadebe! Baba Hadebe!" He turns and looks back .Vaguely he sees a person who is scurrying towards him. He curses again. "Demedi! l blame them again for all this." The man finally catches up with Mr Hadebe. "Good morning Baba Hadebe."

"Oh it's you Mehluli .Good morning. l could hardly make out who was calling me. You know, my other pair of eyes has completely expired. Needless to say l cannot meet the eye examination fee. Neither can I buy a pair of glasses. l am doomed to die in a certain pothole of sightlessness. This is what the authorities have decreed and prescribed for me and a great number of other poor factory workers. We are told lies every day. If lies could fill our stomachs, the severe hunger we are cursed with would be a myth. But daily we are fed with a sea of lies. Lies as green as those nauseous flies which hang around feces. Addressing an important issue like one's sight is now a luxury for us. Perhaps you managers can afford such things".

Mehluli Mdluli clears his throat and sniggers, "Eh... hhh Baba Hadebe. In fact, l should not be embarrassed at all. I am not the author of all this, too .I am a mere victim. Where else in the world have you seen a manager who cannot buy a cough mixture? It can only be here KoMgodo .You could not recognize me, my walk mate because l have a terrible flu. Look at my shoes. Do you honestly think these shoes are appropriate to be owned and worn by a manager?" Mr Hadebe, bends his neck a little low, straining his eyes over Mehluli's feet. Indeed the manager's shoes are a comedy of sole-less fake leather that looks like a giant vessel on the verge of capsizing. The bulges at the front of the shoes are a sure sign that the peeping of toes is imminent. Up the legs old Hadebe sees a pair of black trousers and a patched white shirt, the paleness of colour bearing testimony to the' life' of sunburning they have gone through at a second hands clothes flea market. Both garments are singing the blues of not having had an iron feel for some time now. However, nothing on the young dispatch manager's body more vividly illustrates how a caricature of economic meltdown he has become than the old look on his face. The economic quagmire has ravaged and drained him of any youthful look, leaving behind a trail of accelerated, wizened and elderly air about him.

Mehluli coughs dryly and regards Mr Hadebe as if to say:

The Pair Is Beyond Repair this is now my turn to survey you .The green overalls are dotted with different patches of different colours as if he is a comedian on stage. The farmer shoes he is wearing do not offer any comfort

either to the beholder. The pair is screaming one word: nondescript. Incidentally, Mr Hadebe recalls his last visit to a cobbler who works under a tree. The lanky shoe repairer examined them for thirty seconds before uttering rather slowly." Please feel for them and retire them .I know there is a cancerous tendency here by people, especially leaders being allergic to retirement. I am not saying: condemn and consign it into the bin. But frankly speaking, the pair is beyond repair."

THE ESCAPE ROUTE IN THE DARK

When the elders came up with the adage, 'There is no need to fear a darkness without leopards,' they did not mean the situation which Mr. Bhidliza found himself in...

Once upon a time there lived a very notorious man. He had the beguiling face of a youthful model, guiltless eyes of a tried and tested devout, a beetling chin whose beard looked a little too lengthy and thick for comfort, sometimes priestly, and a handsomely curvy mouth that seemed to mosey, gyrate and beam each time he uttered or smirked.

It is rumoured that some adolescent Hlatshwayo women fetchers of water once exchanged razor-sharp blows at a river well after arguing over the number of times he bathed per day and whether he devoted more time toward making babies than thieving. They were busy shouting obscenities, punching and unleashing fierce and clumsy slaps on each other, when an elderly woman shot on the scene and told them in no uncertain terms that there was no single man on Mother Earth worth fighting for.

Upon being pressed to clarify why he had too many children, he was quick to underline that even the Bible encourages people to proliferate. Whilst the health experts harped on child-spacing, he translated their warnings and had children in different villages! What was no rumour, though, was that women of all ages, colours and sizes fell over themselves for him like his presence had an irresistibly magnetizing effect on them.

It is said that one very dark night, Mr. Bhidliza had snuck into the homestead of a loud-mouthed Member of Parliament. Within seconds, the experienced thief had the honourable Member's classy car cruising at breakneck speed on a bumpy road. Almost as fast as the car took off, it experienced a breakdown. Mr. Gwebu (for that was his real name) alighted from the stolen vehicle, yanked open the bonnet, and was immersed in the gearbox when a female voice emanated from the backseat. He was transfixed. The car he had stolen had a woman occupant in the black cushiony backseat! "Why don't you look at the number plates, SekaNtombi?" Mr. Gwebu shuddered at the question.

He was wondering, How do I deal with this tricky situation now? Is she a witch or something? A ghost? A crazy, homeless drifter? Should I abandon my mission because of this mystery woman? Have I not won over ghosts and other pestering, wandering oddities before? Who is SekaNtombi?

"Why don't you look at the number plates, SekaNtombi? Have we gone past our ancestral cemetery, SekaNtombi?" The female voice came alive again, still addressing him as "father of Ntombi" in the SiNdebele language. His knees squirmed inside his gold designer trousers.

Something greater than panic overwhelmed him as she spoke. It is said a ghostly apparition engulfed and outsmarted him and he tore away, vanishing into distance, into the concentrated darkness that also engulfed him.

* * *

She loved modern technology and modern modes of transport to no end. In the village, most of her neighbours called her 'The Old Woman Who Loves Modern Things in a Nauseating Way.' Her grandson's talkative and assertive wife once told villagers that her grandmother-in law was a "hard-to-love, embarrassing, troublesome, shameless and self-delusional Modern Technology freak." The old lady always strove to keep up with modern technological advancement. She had a Chinese-made, computerized wrist watch, a silver iPad Mini she always admired, and a shiny Samsung Galaxy S2 cell phone that she did not know how to operate. Neither did she know about the mechanics of cars and their body parts.

The old woman had decided to sleep in her grandson's beautiful car because they were to leave early in the morning, at four o'clock sharp, for the City of Gwanda. City of Gwanda, to her, meant modern lights, and hence she was excited. However, she also knew that the chronic government-induced electricity blackouts could mar her stay. She hated all the nation's politicians with a passion, save for her grandson. Most of the country's self-professed prophets and pastors had not endeared themselves to her either. Alone in her hut, more often than not, she would be heard whimpering, "These hypocrites' bodies, including their cursed bones will burn in Hell! They make me s ick!"

Half-asleep in the back of the car, she thought she was talking to her grandson, but what surprised her was that there was no response. In her blissful ignorance it did not occur to her that a mere number plate could not be an issue that could stall a car! The recently awakened old woman is said to have sneezed, salivated and snoozed, then dozed and drooled again; before slipping into a fledged slumber characterized by a dream that gave her an all-seeing role.

An arm-less bearded priest talks in monologues of walking impeccably clean, seeks to scamper away from what looks like a gloomy palace infested with numberless marching disgruntled skeletons and wheezing bees. But along the only path that purportedly leads to the gate of freedom lurks a deep ditch.

The pit is pitilessly dark, maddening and blistering.

The fugitive cleric, heavy-laden with a mountainous loot of gold and silver, cars, cattle and curses, garments and grudges,

women and weaknesses, farcical truths and gossips in place of the gospel of salvation, bribes and brutality instead of bibles and peace, human bones and human odour, and other problematic paraphernalia, literally gropes for the path that leads toward freedom, but slips into the gloomy pit!

Some villagers soon come to the party, and Lord of Lords, she recognises some of them as the chief priests die-hard sycophants and mistresses! She tries to drive them away to no avail as they hurl down one part of a long rope into the abyss for the palace escapee to clinch with his long-matured but tireless and merciless teeth. Up, up the fawning poor pawns pull the tough line.

On the verge of reaching the surface, his thrill of anticipated relief and for continued reign galvanizes him to prematurely utter, "Thank you, com-" and with his horrible heap, he falls tragically back!

Confounded, the old woman woke up. Feeling a startling measure of relief and freedom, she waited in vain until dawn became a verdict that proclaimed she had been stolen as well.

Justice Denied

That's it ...

We exchanged a couple of stinging and hurtful words. In the process I told her in the face that as far as I was concerned she was nothing. Zero, no hero. Nothing!

"Morose moron, you are! No wonder you shore up an archaic party led by a bunch of selfish fuddy—duddies running the country down. How are they different from our cruel former colonizers? They divide and rule. They cater for the needs of their cronies and kin and kith. On one hand they preach peace, on the other they kill mercilessly those who oppose them. They brutalize and degrade. They loot and lie. They only care about their wealth and dynasties and hanging on to power. They are the worst enemies of freedom, human rights and development. They have no compassion for humanity, love for our country; and have no idea about being in strong pursuit of unity, justice and mercy. Warn your party members that they can reel and ruin but the day of reckoning is not far. Joe Girard once said that the elevator to success is out of order. One has to use the stairs...one step at a time. We'II get there. We're paupers. We live under straightened circumstances because of the inefficiency and rapacious behavior of your party officials. They are cruel and abusive, too. Remember the incident of that grandma whose two daughters were forced into a youth militia training camp only to be abused sexually on a daily basis. Upon graduation the two sisters manifested a streak of violence and disobedience galvanized the old woman to strip naked in protest in the presence of the so called trainers and organizers. Look at you, wearing T-shirt bearing the face of another man.

Is that your husband? Crazy fawner! Shame on you Mrs Overzealous!" I slammed her. I wanted her to be repentant and denounce the inglorious acts of violence her party seemed to thrive on.

She frowned at me. The unsightly folds and wrinkles on her face gave me an image of a beautiful tigress whose entrails were being disemboweled in the Hwange Game Reserve. I put it in word. Words sting too. "Umuhle njengempisi ekhanulayo. I mean you smile like a beautiful, beautiful tigress relieving itself happily in the bushes of the Hwange Game Reserve. I pray, I won't have nightmares!' It was her time to fire back. Fire... she spat out sparkles from all the cylinders so to speak. Her voice. It was so hoarse I feared for my precious eardrums. I concluded it stemmed from having taken one bottle too many at a bira (bash) the previous day or had she sung herself to a standstill at the gala?(These galas were a frequent moneygobbling feature of the year in spite of the hyper inflationary conditions under which the ordinary people lived.) She never missed these highly publicized night clubbing and political posturing events of the world as if a fun-loving hobgoblin was upon her. "You've golf clubs for legs. That's why you hobble like an emasculated duck with syphilis. Why you don't seek medical attention eludes me and all common sense! Itch! A bitch times a witch equals you! Mthakathindini wezigodo!" The sneering words sank into my heart as if her spidery fingers were poking my most delicate body parts. I am not belligerent. I felt like exploding all the anger that had gripped me into her. I felt like telling her that even if I were indisposed indeed all the community hospitals and clinics were devoid of the most basic drugs or food. I could not tell her that all the public health institutions were nothing but death traps because all of a sudden I had become inarticulate with anger. There is that bellicose urge to punch sense into a fool's empty head that is synonymous with anger. It is true that an insulated person is disposed to head butt a culprit the Zidane way instantly. I eschewed the temptation in the interest and name of civilization and respect for one's personal rights.

However, in a moment of madness, she spilled some spicy powder on my eyes, spat me in the face. Then she rained punch after punch on my nose, eyes, cheeks, neck, chest and yes you are dead right even on my privates. Yes, l was a recipient of a flurry of punches. I tottered like a drunk, snarled and fell flat. As I lay there in a daze, her booted feet thrust on me, trampling on my stomach, hands and legs. I tried to open my eyes but all I could see were flashing little edgeless stars. If cursing were an index of wealth, then with such people the country wouldn't have been mired in economic quagmire. I was coerced to conclude that she had graduated from an academy for churning out obscenities. Mgodoyi! (cur!).You'll defecate, I'll force you to, pawn thriving on the imperialists' vomit! You will puke! You spineless, senseless gloomy quisling who's always presaging doom. Do you know that I can crush you to death, and no law enforcement officer or court judge would punish me? Don't bullshit me, bitch! Can't you see that the entire country's fucked up! Wake up, you're screwed! I can do literally anything to you under the cover of darkness or during the day, and no person from anywhere or even Mars can protect you!

Yes you can disappear now! Vixen! Witch! You and your other band of malcontents and foreign-driven marionettes, your heads just poke from under the deceivingly warm blankets of white foreigners in our bedroom, backyard, country and what do you do ....? Owing to your obsession with everything about the foreigner, you ejaculate madly in response to his perverted ways, his bloated small house hose pipe spurting out destruction sperms in the form of donor funds, scholarships, donor material donations! You yawn your mouth, your arms, and not to mention your voluptuous legs! Bitch! We're no colony. Shame on you, when we tell you that, you thrust out your head from under the foreign—bought blankets because of his maddening tender sweetness you scream foreign words like democracy and what nonsense. Lizavuka!(You'll wake up). We're deaf when it comes to stupid meaningless foreign lingo!" That's NakaQhude for me, l mean, my next-door neighbor. She beat me up to pulp that Thursday afternoon. An hour later as I lay there wincing, groaning and bleeding until a good Samaritan picked me up and ferried me to Mpilo General Hospital. He later notified my husband about my condition and plight. Luckily my husband brought me some food because the hospital had run out of food supplies. "There is neither a piece of bandage nor a painkiller, mama. I'm told water and power cuts affecting the nation will eventually dog the health institutions. It's possible, mama, who in their wildest dreams could have imagined this major hospital running out of food supplies. In our suburbs every day, water cut, power cut, water cut, power cut, price hikes, shortages and shortages....Oh please this is a serious nightmare. Our beloved country is now a scrapyard of misery. My papers are being processed. I can't stand this. I'm going overseas even it if means doing menial jobs." The whole ward was filled with an aura of desperation and deathly resignation. I drifted into an eerie nightmare... A few meters away from where I stood there was a queue of naked, wailing and chained souls. I saw bloody but skeletal frames of some notorious, living and dead African dictators being struck with an invisible whip, stung by bees and bitten by snakes and termites. One incorrigible Southern African despot was speaking the language of contrition for the first time! I could not believe what I was hearing! Though it was darkish I watched the fat countless colorless bees and termites crawl on their bruised bodies, inflicting pain on their privates, and sometimes disappearing into their anuses and coming out through their yelling mouths. In that seemingly endless queue I also caught sight of some of the most merciless and disreputable European dictators and slave-masters from the Twentieth Century. I heard screams of people confessing to have led lives as deliberate destroyers and distorters of history, architects of slavery and slave trade. Bigots, colonizers, Neocolonizers, oppressors, manipulators, rapists, mercenaries, looters, false preachers, murderers, liars, yes-persons, sell-outs, claimants, charlatans—the list is infinite. Benito Mussolini was denouncing fascist dictatorship. FASCIST DICTATOR were the two words written on his forehead. Adolf Hitler was also screaming for forgiveness. So was imperialist Cecil John Rhodes. However, there was another person who was screaming the loudest. I was shocked to see King Leopold 11 of Belgium whom I had read about in some history books as an admirable philanthropic monarch. He was squealing, "Please, please forgive me for the holocaust I caused!".

With the arrangements of my husband, I was relieved to be taken to a private doctor the following morning, though he had to pay a fortune. Two weeks elapsed and my condition improved considerably.

"You've come to report an assault. You were assaulted two weeks ago, why report now?" asked a police officer whose voice lacked authority and seriousness. I had somehow pulled through. "Vakuru, (Big One) I came two weeks ago and reported the case. You said you had no fuel. You advised me to come with my wife after she had substantially pulled through." My husband explained, worry written all over his charming face. "The accused is Nuza Mpunzi ...? That name rings a bell. What does she do for a living by the way?" "She is a party ward chairwoman. I mean the party ...." I could not complete the sentence because he cut me with fright. "Okay, I see, yes her name is familiar. But .... Ehh ... I think ... well, did she just clobber you from nowhere, for no reason? There must have been some provocation."

The police officers here are known to have a stinking obsession, the syndrome of always seeking to be politically correct. It is not surprising why. In the 1980s when they were carrying out recruitment programs in Bulawayo, they would shamelessly ask candidates whether they were partycard holders and whether their parents were not dissidents. That is how unprofessional, primitive and divisive the security forces were.

"I crossed the floor because of being fed up with that old party's destructive policies, recycled lies, track record and historically infelicitous songs that put emphasis on bloodletting instead of development and respect for the sanctity of life. As a Christian proselyte I quit and she was elevated to ward chairperson after declaring that the operation of destroying the poor people's shacks was welcome and good".

I paused, as if to give him ample time to process the information. After a while I resumed. "She is also going out with a youth leader who is in his late sixties. She grabbed four houses meant to benefit those whose shacks ...."

"Woman, as police, we don't need those stories. You provoked her, right?" I cleared my throat, "No she always pokes fun at me. She tells every person who cares to listen to her that I'm a witch. In my presence she flaunts her party card and she says she has the mother of all fools tucked under her armpit. She admits the child who was playing with my son after dusk was butchered by her party colleagues to enhance their shaky grassroots structures. She is a ritual murderer. But who will believe me even if they carried out the ritual murder because the body of the child was found without a tongue in front of my house?

* * *

On that Thursday afternoon, we were going home after a women's church service when she boasted that the world was convinced I killed a neighbor's child and that I will only get peace, acceptance, repentance and catharsis after rejoining her party. Indignation drove me to tell her that she was no heroine because the iniquities and atrocities of her party will catch up with the culprits. I wanted her to repent and reproach her party officials. For that she scattered some itchy powder over my eyes and punched and kicked me till I passed out. I've a broken index finger and a fractured ...."

"You seem to be recuperating well. Why don't you cut a loss and forget about it? It also smacks of petty jealousies and trivialities associated with political differences...Ah, these useless fights...Now you want to see her punished...Ah... Remember she is powerful and influential. You can end up wallowing in jail for murder. It's possible". My husband was getting impatient. He regarded him sternly and pouted his lips. "Are you going to open a docket or not please? You seem to be meandering or boggling for too long."

"We'll investigate and come to you". That was all he could say in his tired, couldn't careless way of dismissing us. My heart ached. Wounds it felt had not really healed.

It has dragged on and on. It's over a year since that crime was committed and she has not been brought to book. If I had money she could face litigation, the Simpson type of lawsuit. I run into the police on the streets, all I see is partisanship in the execution of their duties. In the sugar or mealie-meal queues the police instead of keeping peace and order, they author disorder and mayhem as they disregard the law abiding citizens and jump the queue with impunity. Last month some courageous women said WOZA (come) here and let us take to the streets because the authorities are sweeping your case under the carpet. Funny enough while we were demonstrating peacefully on the streets, the police all of a sudden had fuel! Some demonstrators dispersed and others were huddled onto the back of police vehicles. Oh talk of the rule of law! Meanwhile, NakaQhude (Nuza Mpunzi), my nextdoor neighbor keeps on bragging about being a sacred cow, a heroine and a true patriot. Mfundisi Dewa prayed for political tolerance the other day, but the problems seem to thicken. He said the country has too many distraught faces and hearts for comfort. Something has to be done.

By the way, NakaQhude and I go to the same church, being stuck in the same burial society, to the same residents association and the problematic price hikes affect us both. It is a pity that the whole thing is so polarized that we no longer see eye to eye. We are no longer on speaking terms in the countless queues we meet because of the political rancor. I look out of the window and see some baton-wielding policemen beating up people for holding an alleged illegal meeting. I wait for justice, and wonder whether they know that justice delayed is justice denied ... or that the next time they heave in sight I would be formally crowned the convenient murder scapegoat? I shudder to think ...

THE INFERNO OF MADNESS

It looks like some mean people have resolved at all costs to take us back to the Dark Ages.

I am sick to the bone about it all. The moment I meet other nationalities and we chit-chat about it, I feel lost, let down and naked. It weighs on my pride, personality and achievements. To be frank, this curse haunts me like a hound. Excruciating bruises are written all over me, all over my place and conscience. It is a shattered dream that haunts me day in and day out. It is so mind-boggling that it clouds the horizons of my imagination and determination.

By the way, the other day I sneaked out of my office while my immediate boss, who since morning had been either reading the foreign newspaper or phoning his friends overseas- was dozing off and frothing on the mouth. I was not sneaking out because I was on the verge of throwing up. The elders have a saying: the one (meaning the eagle) that soars about has a chance of catching (probably a chick). And so like a roving eagle, I bumped into my former neighbor who is affectionately if not notoriously referred to as Mr. Patriot Anarchy. He is now a "salad" or one of those who live in the low density suburbs. Talk of privileged consumers of fish salad, cheese salad or vegetable salad. l am still a "tshwalala",a bastardized term for those who live in "townships" and mainly rely on thick maize porridge for sustenance. For the majority of the low density suburbans who have no constant supply of groceries from those in the Diaspora, even to talk of eating salads would tantamount to lying through the teeth. Hunger rules supreme whether one is a rustic dweller or a town fellow. The farmers they chased away from the land are in neighboring countries and overseas. Does it make sense to kick out productive farmers, and the next thing you are seen in those "unwanted" countries where these "unwanted" people are, and what are you doing there? And it turns out you are actually begging for money and mercy, of course? You chase away the farmers, and then sooner than later you follow them to import food from the very countries these agricultural people producing? Who is delusional and demented here? Who has the last laugh? Please, come on, get real! These are precious people's lives and destinies we are discussing here. Bread and butter issues. Get a life or get a boot. The people are calling for the scalps of all bigoted bunglers.

Their shamelessness is sickness. Come to think of it, whenever the ruling party members have a platform and an opportunity to air their views on the state of affairs, they either paint a rosy picture of things, or claim the government is committed to solving some of the sticky situations. They even go on and say people should be patient and patriotic. If it were that simple, they should be leading by example. We would not have dropped to these miserable economic and social levels as a country if they were patriotic, serious and knew what they were doing in the first place. If the schools and universities are still well-staffed and well-equipped, and the educational standards have not fallen down as they claim is the case, why do they send their children to educational institutions outside the country? Now the real patriotic and patient ordinary people are writing petitions to the relevant institutions and governments to have these students deported. What a circus! It is the same story with health institutions. They have failed to maintain hospitals and whenever they fall sick, they fly out. At whose expense? At the taxpayer's, of course. Who are they fooling by preaching their fake gospel of patriotism? Love for this mineral-rich country, my foot!

Back to Mr. Anarchy. Upon catching sight of me, he teased: "Hunger has a way of making people fat like pigs." I reluctantly shook his rough and greasy hands and responded, "Pigs eat everything. The elders say nobody knows what made pigs fat. But here there is nothing to eat, even my bones are emasculated. There is no cruelty and witchcraft worse than this!" You know what he said upon being questioned why he was putting on a few kilos in the middle of a desert of basic food shortages? He smiled, revealing teeth which were not yellowish from relentless pulls of the cigarettes, but the foulness of his breath epitomized the patent effects of a long concluded divorce between his mouth and any form of toothpaste.

"I know you have slunk out of the office to join one of those endless stale bread queues! The police, as you know, respect no queue. Sometimes if you are lucky to get a loaf, you would have to be battle with a constipation problem or a running tummy." I added rather cautiously," The police in this country promote corruption and disorder. And you may be tempted to keep your mouth shut for fear of emitting stale aroma!" I saw him subconsciously or intentionally muffle his mouth with his right hand.

In response to my aforementioned question, words of finality he delivered with a renewed zest and zeal." As long as queues keep on snaking and shortages persist, I prosper, for in confusion I surely prosper. I prosper under dubious and opaque circumstances, I thrive well under the shadow of darkness. I used to have meetings with the sons and daughters of Mr Inflation, but now during the day or night l mingle and mix with Mr Inflation Senior. I mean Sir Hyper-inflation!"

That is Mr. Anarchy for you. The man who decided to lose his soul and senses in pursuit of a life of spreading lies and confusion in the name of keeping the ruining party's leader and his shenanigans, doing what they know best-ruining first and ruling for ever and ever amen. This is the same lousy praise singer l told in the face a few months ago to go hang on Mount Party Marionettes, and fall headlong with all the king's acolytes ready to sing songs of heroic patriotism (instead of blatant partisanship)-after declaring his sexual lust for me. He actually whispered to me sensually, "Night is right for this. I will be your moon to give you a series of unforgettable moans". I was not going be a sex object for him or any other man in this man-made hell. I told him to go to hell and burn in eternity. My words stung him into silence. In fact, he looked like a hot-water doused cock! His colleagues preach powerful and sorrowful messages about the importance of fidelity in the face of the AIDS pandemic year in year out, yet most of them are busy buying concubines and mistresses with money meant for poor AIDS patients.

Not to mention that they have contributed significantly in a -couldn't- care- less -attitude to the total collapse of the health system. There is a rapid deterioration of the health service delivery system, lack of adequate water supply, and lack of capacity to dispose of solid waste and repair sewage blockages in most areas. All these in-capacities continue to contribute to the escalation and spread of many contagious diseases. The selfish leaders are not worried to death. Why? Because they are out of touch with the rest of the citizens. Because they can fly out of the kingdom at the slightest scream of their bulging stomachs, or when their imported groceries run out.

The dream. All shattered. The brave sons and daughters of the struggle paid the supreme price, deep in their hearts and heads were treasures of regaining dignity, land and their rights as citizens. Their songs were loud and clear, harping on freedom of association, press freedom and other tenets of democracy. The blood-thirsty emperor has made a mockery of Prince Franchise. This is a very sad state of affairs because all the sons and daughters of Mr. Scam and Mrs. Sham (or is it Shame?) take center whenever ballot time comes. These sons and daughters team up with such dirty-minded people like Mr. Anarchy and run roughshod over Prince Franchise. I am bleeding in my heart as l report that Sir Democracy has gone AWOL. I heard him with my ears. I shall only return when there is sanity. Those were his words before he escaped. There is a humanitarian, political, social and economic catastrophe that should galvanize the decent souls to put their heads together and seek a lasting solution. But...l do not know. Economic meltdown is taking its toll. Political rape is suffocating and submerging all the voices of reason and dissent. It is a disgrace. I mean a calamity plus a bottomless pity. I am outraged.

Friend, this is an open secret. The emperor and Sir Democracy are like oil and water. You know what, Sir Democracy was on the minefield the very moment he declared no person had a right to foist hunger, penury and dehumanization on the poor in the name of promoting and protecting autocracy for eternity. Sir Democracy, being frank and open as his is-thoroughly rapped the emperor and the royal cronies for dining and wining without a care on the innocent blood of our fallen heroes and heroines. He also slammed His Majesty for brutalizing Prince Franchise and all the people who supported the prince. The bootlickers did not mince their words, they said he was treading where angels fear. Call to mind, those people have made it their duty to feel' pain' for him, and if it were possible, they would cough and cringe for him!

I look up to Sir Democracy. I doff my hat to Prince Franchise. Both epitomize our struggle for dignity, freedom and normalcy. l also salute Miss Equality. One dark night, the so-called Owls visited her. She was battered and insulted for exercising her constitutional right to express her views and opinions .One royal member attempted to rape her, and for all his troubles she kicked his testicles nice and fast, Will Smith style until he passed out! Actually, the dazed culprit put his fingers between his legs, as if to prove whether the "kitchen utensils" were there or there was no more ball to be played!

Later, as assertive as ever, she told people attending a residents meeting that only idiotic women went into paroxysms of jubilation and praise singing after being given a mere piece of meat before an election. Hunger stalks the land for the majority, but a certain dish of fish called propaganda does not run out. Hardly a day passes by without one watching those gigantic fish on TV. These vertebrate cold blooded animals with grills are portrayed by the overzealous bootlickers as real and nutritious.

Miss Equality was arrested for writing in the local paper that what people were actually hearing was nothing but verbal diarrhea. She was castigated for saying there is a lot of hand-clapping, handshaking, pontificating or posturing whilst the kingdom was going up in flames. She said the country was under siege from mindless and merciless bigots, sexual predators, misogynists, strongmen and bootlickers. I was moved by her words that day. "Brothers and sisters, speak out. Homophobic bigots, sexual predators, misogynists, dictators and kiss-asses have to be kicked out. Give all of them the boot they deserve if the rot has to be wiped out. All these misfits don't deserve to be anywhere near an office of leadership and authority. They don't deserve your votes and respect either. Whistle-blow. Name all the beneficiaries of this rotten system, too. Shame the shameless and smelly ass-kissers of the despotic leaders. Tell the world your story. Don't wait for a Moses to descend from heaven. Tell yourself you are your own Moses. Did not our wise elders say: the Rock Rabbit has no tail because of his dependence on the generosity of others? Similarly, didn't our seniors warn us about a thing that belongs to someone else? They did. They said a thing that belongs to someone else is the gravy of the hyena. Just as our African liberators fought and saw the vanquishment of white colonialism, we must fight and defeat modern colonialism, fascism, prejudice, dictatorship and corruption." Upon meeting her in the food queues people ululated, chanting" Our Lady Moses. True! A plough that belongs to someone else cannot banked on for a good harvest. If a tyre has a puncture, what do we do? You would say: mend the tyre. If a soccer coach is giving fans no joy but a series of failures and excuses, what do we do? Yes, we show the bungler the red card! Th e exit!"

Master Corruption would hear no word of it, though he is the official way of conducting business here. He called Miss Equality names like-poisonous witch and uncultured, westernized street-girl. Master Corruption actually leapt in the air like a possessed herbalist hit his chest five times and declared no Western-indoctrinated woman should talk as if she has what men have between their legs! There was uproar as some bold women demonstrated in the streets. All of them were bundled into the back of a truck and detained in a prison whose toilets were flushed once per week- for two months, eating maize porridge once a day.

As a woman, I look at the innocent children whose future has been ruined and tears start to cascade down my cheeks. There has to be a better life. Is this a life, really? Do we deserve all these debasing experiences? It suits us well? What about the children whose future has been turned into doom and gloom? What sin have they committed? Their schools are nothing but some white elephant. There is no schooling to talk of unless if one can afford to pay a 'private' tutor in foreign currency for extra lessons. The hospitals and clinics are devoid of any form of medication under the sun. No pill. No nothing. Absolutely horrifying institutions. No longer life-saving centres. Not anymore. People just pray that they do not fall sick. How precarious a life this is. And cholera is always lurking. It is and was always coming...No wonder, for where are the chemicals to treat the water? Innocent people are dying like flies. Yet there is always money for rallies to demonize the opposition, the West and for flying overseas to pontificate about our 'independence and successes' as a people! And the world listens... or does it?

Then there are the senseless killings and a wave of violence, fear, indoctrination, discrimination and intimidation? Who shall put out this inferno of madness? The players? Are they not putting their selfish and personal agenda ahead of the plight of the majority? My hope will not perish in the midst of this suffering, and the collapsing of the kingdom. Somebody else? No. I am a woman of strength, endurance and with a vision. Just as the fallen heroes and heroines had a dream, I also need to dream anew. It is real most of my countrymen are scattered all over the world. It is also real that there is no currency to talk about in this kingdom, something people call 'burial' checks (meaning the real money has been laid to rest in the cemetery of corruption or something!) To make matters worse, banks time and again run out of those useless but numerous papers.

I personally shall not whimper, but do something about this decay, this conflagration, this stench and this imprisonment. My home land has been turned into a kingdom of muddle, misery and madness, but I have a burning desire to transform it into a heaven of hope, prosperity and unity. This rebuilding and healing process starts with me. National radio and TV stations are powerful media houses. But these are rooted on one side of the coin. Is it possible that all the people who are interviewed there think alike? No, the question should be-what can or should I do? I will tell my story with vigor irrespective of all the indignities I have suffered. For the African proverb spells it out: until the lions get their own historian the tale of the hunt will always glorify the hunter.

THE FIVE-STAR HONEYMOON HORROR

There is always a first for everything. Mr. Lungile Dube and Mrs. Sukoluhle Dube thought as they made efforts to book directly with the hotel online. The lovebirds, lovingly and habitually called each other *Lu* or *Lungi* and *Su* or *Suko* respectively. Lungile means the *good one* while Sukoluhle means *good day*. They had met four years ago and had not looked back till they tied the knot.

If Sukoluhle always thought her Prince Charming, her Knight in shining amour of the zebra totem was the quintessence, classification and embodiment of the goodness of love for her, Lungile had no doubt on his mind that Sukoluhle, who was of the elephant totem and from the Gatsheni household, was born on this planet to brighten up his days and his heart as his big beautiful royal queen. Her maiden name was Sukoluhle Ndlovu, hence sometimes he called her MaNdlo, the Elephant Queen. Such calling or labeling and nicknames lightened up and warmed up things like a little fire in wintertime. The given names gave them some kind of stimulation, titivation and elation. They fired up and tickled their frame of mind, love, situations and hearts in a special fashion into a supportive, active and constructive chat, joke or laughter in spite of the vagaries of the weather and the lows and highs of any given relationship and the rigors, turns and tides of life itself. On their wedding day, one of the elderly speakers had lectured them on the beauty and bliss of love. He admonished them to keep on rekindling their love. He said love is a fire that has to be refuelled in order to conquer all. He also touched on the power of positivism and calmness in the face of negative dynamisms and adversities. Adversities stalk our landscapes, our lives and love. But like impurities, they have to be reined in or removed.

They searched online for a five-star hotel, for a list of desired amenities, for the availability of accommodation, for a gateway to fun, love, laughter and luxury. It had to be right and out of this world: their honeymoon excursion, their stay. *Honeybun, your happy hubby is saying: today it's our delight. Our love is all the light we need. Right?* Lungile asked rhetorically. No doubt, love was in the air. Love roared and ruled.

On the other hand, when they got there, the reception was manned by a dozy, tipsy, tubby, filthy fella who thought he was amazing and amusing by prating: *your room's a lovely lovers' haven, you're free to scr...eeech yourselves to a soothing, startling and shameless climax but...but don't wake up some of our quiet guests, remember hotels don't know, screen and turn away serial murderers, maniacs, drug addicts, drug traffickers, dangerous drunkards, human traffickers, rapists, pickpockets, ladies of the night and ghosts! We are warm and welcoming. Yes, always happy and hospitable. For ours is a hospitality industry. Enjoy!*

Was it a malfunctioning cord, missed connections, a WiFi router interference with the TV, a lighting situation , a seating arrangement problem ,a disabled energy efficiency function , overheating or dying bulbs that the plasma TV in the room was acting up like a sullen soul ,causing a very annoying ,fooling ,flickering glitch? At the back of the heads of Lungile and Sukoluhle were puzzled and pondering thoughts and questions like: *It doesn't look like a very old device. Is the system for converting visual images into electrical signals moody and faulty? Maybe it's on some kind of silly hunger strike and has downed its tools of entertainment, education and information. Hope we aren't in for a rude awakening here.*

For instance, as soon as they entered the room, it dawned on them that the unsightly, moldy walls were a loud, shamed echo of tear-and-wear, marijuana smoke and blood stains. They had bullet holes too. It was a crammed or squalid building. A raving mad, reeking rathole. The ceiling looked silly with all sorts of cracks that cracked no joke. The smell of cigarette smoke invaded their nostrils as if a device in the vicinity had an electrical or mechanical problem field day. They wondered. *Is there something overheating? Won't it catch fire? Lord! Could this sudden and unexplained smell be emanating from that ill-omened flickering television set?*

If the front desk's man's antics were a complete circus of mannerisms, the butler services were as nonexistent as the door that would not lock, the window that rudely, raucously and seemingly looked them in the eye and refused to close, the air conditioner that was on hiatus indefinitely, the flopping elevators, the blinding red lights that made their blood-stained room look eerie and creepy, the high-speed internet WiFi which nailed how to process data at the speed of a tired, frail snail. As things stood, it was clear to the couple that their honeymoon was unfolding in front of their naked eyes like a huge horror movie. Nothing was working well for them. *Poor Wifi, respect our honeymoon. We want to live stream our momentous event and spread love and glee.*

Don't be a sick and senseless spoiler. She carped. Mrs Sukoluhle Dube was not impressed. Neither was her Dube Knight in shining amour.

They shared the room with a battalion of giant, jiving, daring and disobedient rats. Not only that. It was a happy haven for spiders, beetles, cockroaches and bedbugs. As if all that were not enough nightmare, one-gun carrying man with a swollen, scarred and scary face, red and roaming eyes stormed into their room. Lungile was visibly shaken. Sukoluhle mutely and suddenly prayed for the day's shift into bliss and brightness, something they were there for. She was eagerly waiting to whisper sweet nothings into the ears of Lu, her Lungi.

The very second he opened his mouth, the presence, prevalence and power of his breath seemed resolute to instantly induct and plunge them into a pool of intoxication. The smell of his breath captured the entire room. That they could smell alcohol on his breath was no debate. It was a non-issue to argue over. It simply required a minimum of thought. It were as if his lungs were busy tributaries into his kind of Limpopo River, into which alcohol was lavishly and habitually absorbed. Perhaps alcoholic scent produced by his pores could get one tipsy! *He is a moving cocktail bar, one can possibly get drunk by merely shaking hands with him*, she assumed. Did the intruder look like a character who cared a whit about his body stink? About getting the beer smell off his breath?

"Hi guys, seen my girlfriend? Tall, tottering, stark-naked and totally sloshed? The thing is she whacked and punched me like a crazy virago. I'm not ashamed to admit that she kicked my big blameless balls really hard, so hard l passed out". He paused as if he were running out of breath. They did not know whether to feel sorry for him or to pass a remark. What they knew at that point in time was to tread cautiously. They knew too that it was not a good idea to wade into his story. The backlash could be absurd, impulsive and inconceivable. The truth of the matter was that they just wanted him to get the hell out of their sight, their hotel room.

He resumed, "Then she staggered out, probably looking for a hideout. She won't get away with it, and those who try to shield her. The bottom line is that I want her back: naked or clad, dead or alive. They don't call me SSK for Senior Serial Killer for nothing. Where's she? Seen her? Do you want me to describe her hairiness or lack of it, or her nipples?"

If he looked like a decent and pleasant character, what was spiraling out of his mouth could have raised their eyebrows. But then he looked neither decent nor pleasant. It is said that good poetry enables the reader to observe, hear, feel, touch, taste, smell or see what the poet experienced when he or she poetized or composed his or her piece of poetry. The study or analysis of their poetry was a piece of upsetting poetics. For instance, what they had already experienced, observed, felt, touched and smelt was enough to drive a normal person cracked. The last thing they wanted to hear was a hippie droning on how nice or what his girlfriend's nipples were or how dense or plain her body looked like. *Oh please, please, for heavens' sake, spare us that garbage, we have had a maddening mountain and drama of pranks, peculiarities and agonies by now.* They seemed to protest peacefully to themselves. Lungile was of the opinion that his wife had the nicest nipples on this earth, what he called the lovely and loving ripples he loved and longed to breeze and queeze with his fervent fingers and healing hands. He was not interested in listening to the description of nipples of some fooling fugitive who was capable of kicking a man's manhood into castration and incapacitation.

Barefooted, the intruder was clad in body-hugging spermstained blue briefs that seemed to reveal what they were expected to conceal and an undersized whitish, terribly tiny vest whose lousy length struggled to cover his navel, let alone his waist. The sight of the man and the twist of his story sent shivers down their spines. Though the last question was as ridiculous as the appearance and conduct of the trespasser, they could not laugh. It was no joke. It was no laughing matter either. Both Lungile and Sukoluhle had lived long enough to realise that such characters were lousy and loose cannons and nuisances. The world was not yet free from unpredictable prowlers and pests. Predators have a tedious and terrible tendency of preying on the innocent members of any given society. Wherever there are predators, danger lurks.

Therefore both Lungile and Sokuluhle responded almost at the same time, "No...No!" One could have wondered: were they saying no, they had not seen her undressed girlfriend or they were saying no to his wish to describe her nipples? It was an interesting idea to explore. However, for the couple, nothing was interesting about their ordeal. If they were not on top of their game, their honeymoon was topsy-turvy. That was the sad state of affairs. The Dubes were drowning in a state of confusion and frustration. There was no time for cracking jokes, for throwing around words of encouragement and love . There was no time for playing around with their nice nicknames. What a test. It was dire. *How will this drama unfold and end*? *Life is such a ....* They looked at each other in utter bewilderment and disappointment. Their lips and eyes were dotted and decorated with ellipses and question marks. They pinched their skins. No, it was not a dream. They did not deserve that ordeal. That drama was playing out on the day of their honeymoon. How dare, drama! A day that was expected to be special, delightful and remarkable. Hell no, why? However, they had no choice but to be positive and prayerful. Positivity is a psychological, physical and spiritual weapon, leverage and compass which can x-ray, penetrate and terminate barriers and trials.

He gawked at the couple as if, at that point in time, he would point his gun at the two panicky and pensive lovebirds and empty its mad and malicious contents on them. Nevertheless, he kissed his gun and offered them cannabis. "OK, guys, it's my pleasure to invite you to partake in this herbal feast that will leave you high in the sky and happy. Want to burn it with a bang?"

Lungile prayed that the strange man would not harm his spouse. The man was a harassing sight. However, he wished he could get his wife away from harm's way. Though he was a peaceful, thoughtful and harmless- looking husband, even in fear , he was not ready and willing to abdicate his natural and cultural role of being her motivator, pillar, protector and provider. Let that stranger not touch his better half. He was prepared to defend her at any cost and at any place and time. You mess with an enraptured and enamoured man's partner at your expense, they say. He can turn the tables on someone else when people least expect him to. Even the weakest and cowardliness man becomes the toughest, bravest and meanest soul where matters of the heart are concerned, so said and cautioned the elders. He wanted to take measured steps. Not rushed and irrational ones.

Their plane of love had a gun-toting hijacker. If they were the victims, he was their captor. They could not afford to throw caution to the wind. Hence, they guardedly, respectfully and tensely turned him down. Good Heavens! The sight was a horrendous dream. He went on a rampage of kicking and miskicking anything and everything he could lay his feet and eyes on. His private bodily parcels drooped, danced and peeped out as he pounced on guiltless possessions and paraphernalia. *Maybe those precious possessions thought he was possessed.*

He kicked and upturned the plastic rubbish bin; burped, slurred and snarled a volley of f-prefixed obscenities, oddities and threats before teetering out. Fortunately, their bodies were spared from his hell of kicks and miskicks. They had not seen or heard someone belch like that before. And the accompanying and added *perfume*...? It could hound and heave a thief out of his or her hideout with an alarming degree of suffocation and inebriation. Was his tummy always that terrifyingly rebellious and boisterous too?

The unhappy but relieved honeymooners promptly sat on the floor, prostrated, raised their hands, lowered their heads; and whispered quick spiritual introspections, pleas, praises, cheers and sighs, and stood up, packed and darted out to the front desk. There they demanded a refund and hit the road and drove away to saneness, safety and positivity.

The Bambazonke Syndrome

The little history I know about Aunt NakaThembelihle is that she was a school teacher and an activist of sorts.

She taught both in the urban and rural areas of the country. During her active years in education and after retirement she advocated for the protection and promotion of the youth, chiefly those infected by AIDS, or with albinism; or the abused. She used to watch nearly 100% of Highlanders matches in Zimbabwe.

Aunt NakaThembelihle visited us a few days ago, what a lively chat we had over a number of issues. Dynamic as ever, she told me how she used to support her favorite soccer club through its lows or highs. What strike me is the fact that she is an old lady who follows what is happening around the country in particular and the world in general. A nonagenarian, she still exhibits a measure of smartness in terms of observational skills in spite of her poor sight and diabetic state.

Of all the three daughters of my aunty, none is a nurse but she is disheartened by the government's recent decision to sack 15 000 nurses for engaging in a strike action. "I've always stood with those in dire straits, in destitution, in distress, those whose plight and grievances are ignored or brushed aside.

I supported the liberation war fighters for the same reason.

Today, I stand in solidarity with the dismissed nurses. *Nx* !"

A frequent visitor to the myriad of the country's public health bodies, she believes paralysis has turned them into death traps. "In the past, do you know that Luveve Clinic had specialists and all the equipment and drugs you could think of? Now, it's sad, big hospitals like Mpilo are devoid of basic drugs! On social media, you see sickening, bragging, conscienceless and heartless beneficiaries and scoundrels of this rotten system flaunting their latest pricy top of range cars, mansions, garments and jewelry. You then expect nurses and doctors who are underpaid, under-equipped to work as if everything's fine. That's clowning. Where's sanity?"

She said everybody has a right to life and a fair trial, not what she called the Bambazonke Games which we are being exposed to on a daily basis. "What do you mean, auntie?" I inquired. "I've never been a big fan of the Bambazonke mentality. It's delusional. It's a self-serving mentality which falsely assumes that one has a right to grab everything, anywhere, anyhow. A win-win affair for oneself without compromises. It breeds a false sense of entitlement and pride."

We discussed sports again, only this time she was telling me how proud over the years she has been of the performances and pedigree of the national cricket team. "Your cousin, Thembelihle who has lived in India and other countries says when foreigners introduce cricket as a subject for discussion she looks them in the eye, and takes them head-on. Why? It's one of the few sports in which we've made a name for The Bambazonke Syndrome ourselves". She paused for a while, as if she waiting for me to weigh in on topic. Aunt NakaThembelihle had her own way of broaching subjects. A fearless and frank lioness, she was.

She concluded, "On that note, I stand with Health Streak, our cricket legend. Our son of the soil whose fluency in Ndebele is our source of joy and pride. Is he not the only Zimbabwean cricketer to have taken more one hundred ODI wickets? Does he not hold the record for the most five wicket hauls by a Zimbabwean? Is he not our finest ever bowler? Hmm... I smell a scapegoating hand of the Bambazonke syndrome .Hope cricket won't be the loser".

Aunt NakaThembelihle always made me believe that she carried the pains, stories and burdens of the voiceless, browbeaten and disenfranchised members of our communities. She told the untold stories of grief that cried with the victims' souls for relief and closure. For the annihilation of hegemony, hatred and hell. For a freer, happier, healthier and safer society.

THE HAPPY HEADMAN'S DRAMATIC MONOLOGUE

It's not *old news* that Methuseli lived remotely close to two neighbors whose unneighborliness was amusing. The two were biologically related in a distant fashion.

Then their wives were *found missing* on their farms, not that they had decided to go to another planet and become resident aliens, but because they had to dig up a well in an almost exactly water less river. Their faces wore *clear confusion* since portable water seemed to be nowhere to be found or simply elusive. Legend has it that dryness danced down the river the moment the villagers chased away a mermaid.

Certainly, it could be that they spent futile fourteen hours there, and their *overbearingly modest* and *understanding* men would not understand it a bit! Methuseli was not only one of the villagers there but also was a humble headman who *climbed down* a step or two and availed and offered his services to the community members with poise and pride.

"People should learn to live in harmony in this village. The *only choice* the two of you have is to either leave our village or to live in peace. Is this *clearly understood*?" An eloquent and earsplitting silence descended on the scene. Indeed, both the Moyos and Dlomos screamed silent squeals.

Both accused the headman of cruel kindness, and both were *openly deceptive* because they did not wear sad smiles and did not tell him that he was exhibiting *caring cruelty*. "Your silent screams mean that you're either living dead or are loyally opposed to my intervention and jurisdiction. I mean, l know that I'm not mean. Either way, the difference is the same, just get a life and be extinct if you're not going to listen to me, the chief's envoy!"

Both families wondered whether they were icy hotheads and wise morons seeking to find the meaning of life in an island surrounded and punctuated with a sea of meaninglessness.

They pondered whether they were merely clever fools whose life was nothing but a web of confusions, convolutions and conflicts, an array of oxymoron's, ironies and paradoxes. Where were life's formulas, manuals, templates, trajectories and prescriptions? Were they not like learner drivers bearing the letter L when it came to living and making sense of life, its highs and lows, turns and twists?

What makes one glad doesn't necessarily make the other person contented. What heals one patient doesn't essentially cure the next person. Right? What angers one soul sometimes pleases the other. What is one's preferred plate is another guzzler's spurned pollution. What is one's success story is another person's fiasco or mediocrity. Even words like development and democracy mean different things to different people. One man's issue is another's no- issue. Such is life. A bulky ball and breath of colours, creeds, complexities, contradictions, controversies, consensuses and corrections. Feats, flaws and failings. Different people have different perspectives and perceptions.

Certainly, life is a gift to be cherished, cared-for and celebrated. It is a celebration of stars, the days, the moments and the opportunities. An embracing of love, friendships, families, funniness, foolishness, the beauty of the breeze, the marveling of the moon, the sun and the vastness and uniqueness of the sky.

Of seeking peace of mind, stability and compromises even in the face of silent screams, right wrongs, virtuous liabilities, uninvited urgings, dressed transparencies, unstable sanities, static flows of impossible solutions, easy riddles, blissful elegies, painless pains, bright nights, dark days and genuine imitations. It is a bold stride in spite of repellant pulls and unruly, noisy serenity. Life is a legacy. A mysterious, matchless march towards nobility and exceptionality.

It turned out to be a turning point for the two families whose nights had *working vacations*, whose bodies had restless, sleepless calm by virtues of being locked in frequent friendly battles of tossing live snakes and truthful lies at one another, that day was a dawn and an end, they swore a silent, stern and sane vow to live life awfully good the way they knew how. Life had to be lived, relearned and relished.

"You are no longer the *original copies* of children. Yet your actions indicate that you're *growing smaller and shorter* likeburning candles. At least, burning candles give out light. You don't! Irresponsible responsibility or unbehaving behavior won't be tolerated here. We don't allow *adult children* to live in this village. Kids, yes. Hope your deafness has heard, for it has to heed". The headman concluded.

Seeking Refuge

Messages come in many shapes, sizes and colors but what is crucial is how we interpret and implement them.

If friendships, relationships or marriages were scripted like plays and movies, life would not be as dramatic and enigmatic as we know it to be. We write and practice our scripts as we live, love and transition.

I love the sky. How magic it is to marvel at that celestial dome as it towers above the Earth. I begin to visualize daylight and the delight of sightseeing birds and insects as they fly in their sky; l bask in the cordiality and cuddle of the sun, and wander away in a trance into the wonder of the clouds, lightning and rainbows before arriving at the constellations; l then go clubbing with the night and its stars, and the moon (though the stars hog the limelight!); finally l decide to hang out with precious Precipitation's dear family and friends, l mean lovely and lively chaps like Rain, Hail, Drizzle, Sleet and Snow.

What fun! No company beats their watery warmth, harmonies and hospitality, l swear!!

I love the wilderness in the form of wild animals, forests, vegetation, rocks, rivers and beaches. These amazingly beautiful things go about their business despite human intervention. Bravo!

People, the preservation of the universe — which is the natural, physical, or material world—is essentially the preservation of life, and this cause is close to my heart.

NO EXERCISE IN FUTILITY BUT THE FUTURE

The Mohammed Bushera story is a story of perseverance, possibilities and posterity. A story of heroism, humanity, help, honesty, health and happiness. Perhaps for someone who has never ever delved into some kind of a regular and well-thought-out physical fitness programme like some forms of yoga, the mere thought of embarking on such a potentially life-changing and lifesaving journey could be a daunting deterrent.

Questions abound: Where and when does one begin or get cracking, and can one become and stay physically fit? *Are the youth seized with the business of choosing, adopting, attaining and sustaining a healthy, happy and proactive lifestyle by keeping themselves physically fit and focused, emotionally and spiritually stable*? What about the amount of time, energy, funds, fun and tools one has to invest into this physical training and process? How soon is the turnaround time? Do human beings not find pleasure and pride in seeing and experiencing results *as soon as yesterday's gig*? Do people not tend to be more goal-orientated than process-patient? Is a shortcut not always the in-thing— our fastest lane to rewards, realization and relief? After all, patience is a virtue.

Is one fit, disciplined and devoted enough to swing and sweat into a fruitful fitness routine in style? Would one manage and cope with a combination of a moderate and strict, vigorous— intensity activity spread throughout the week? What about monetary and dietary changes? Is it easy or stress-free to leap out of one's comfort zone? For example, to ditch junk stuff for healthy food? Do we always pause and ponder the monetary and dietary consequences of our actions and eating habits? Do we always have a careful weighing of our actions or inactions on issues of health and happiness? How often do we ponder the course of an action or inaction? It is not an ultimate battle of decisions and indecision's, doubts and confidence, faults and flawlessness? The fear of fear itself, or of being judged or failing?

Does one need to be a bodybuilder, a boxer or an athlete to build muscle strength and endurance? By the way, muscle strength and endurance is one of the key elements of physical fitness. Strength training is a significant constituent of an overall fitness programme. Strength training is self-explanatory because it seeks to reinforce or strengthen one's muscles and bones, and to keep the heart and lungs strong. It promotes weight and protects one against chronic disease.

What forms of exercise confer various rewards or advantages, which in turn, can help one balance the different elements of physical fitness? What if one does not have an inkling of the different types of strength and their benefits?

How does one meet fitness standards in all four categories? Strength training usually involves the use of resistance bands, resistance machines, free weights and other tools—what if one does not have such equipment? Does one have to pay for a gymnasium membership or costly equipment to strengthen one's muscles and bones? Why broach this subject? Is an act of avoiding it altogether not equivalent to seeking a stress-free life?

A 28 –year old businessman –Mr. Mohammed Bushera, who runs a small shop (one that would pass for or could be accepted as a tuck shop or a spaza shop in South Africa) because it heavily houses and hawks small everyday household items in Kirkos, Woreda 2, Kebele 3, Addis Ababa in Ethiopia – boldly begs to differ. "No, it isn't? In fact, exercise reduces stress! Lack of finance or equipment shouldn't be a deterrent. Seek creative solutions to these challenges I'm a living testimony to that reality. One has to be creative, active, positive and improvise. For instance, make use of one's space, time and homemade weights. A bit of organized physical activity is better than none." By the way, a *woreda* is an administrative division of Ethiopia which is essentially managed by a local government while a *kebele* is a small administrative unit.

His determination is disarming and deserving of mention, ovation and recognition. Here is an inspirational young man whose life can possibly be transformed through mentorship, financial sponsorship, empowerment or technology. His level of responsibility, ingenuity and grit has a measure of merit to it. Indeed, over a period of three years on my way to work, I have had the blessing, privilege and honor of watching him humbly and hungrily work out early in the morning, in whatever weather and with the plainest of equipment like a recycled car tyre ,a rope or a set- up of logs . Yet he has forged ahead and physically changed for the better and impacted society in a positive and progressive fashion. He normally gets down to business while music from either Nigeria or South Africa looms, booms and belts out of his small speaker. He exercises outside his business building, sweating it out profusely yet his strong work ethic gives an observer an image of a celebrant who could be having the happiest of holidays or moments. His bold actions bear testimony to the fact that a lack of resources is not necessarily a lack of dynamism, dedication and focus.

What drove him to exercise? He chuckles, "For starters, I'm business-minded. Exercise is key to one's mental and emotional being. I wanted to be healthy and happy. I wanted to show those who don't have much, especially the youth that it can be done. Africa, it can be done. Don't be idle. Exercise. Exercising isn't an option. It's a must." On the ground, I have no shred of doubt that he is now an exemplary source of devotion, inspiration and positivity in the community. Now and then, passers-by: adults and schoolchildren alike stop by and marvel at his level of commitment and creativity. Exercise changes the body, the mind, the mood and attitude for the better. As little as 30 minutes of moderate exercise per day is beneficial, so advise the mental health and physical fitness doyens and advocates.

What constitutes a rounded exercise programme? In general, the four essential elements of physical training are: cardiorespiratory endurance, muscular strength and endurance, flexibility, and maintaining a healthy body composition. Each part offers precise health benefits, but best health calls for some degree of balance between all the four categories.

Experts believe that one convenient and innovative instrument for putting together an exercise plan is the FITT acronym. FITT stands for: *frequency* –how often does one exercise? For instance, Mr. Bushera exercises three times per week in front of his shop. *Intensity*—how hard one works during one's exercise session? *Time*—how long does one exercise for? *Type*—what kind of exercise does one do? For example, Mr. Bushera does weight-lifting, leg squats, abdominal crunches, push-ups and press-ups. Aerobic activities like jogging, walking or jogging fall under cardiorespiratory endurance. So is biking, and ...talk of killing two birds with one stone since the use of bikes and recycled car tyre is not only in aid of issues of health and happiness, but also climate change! Climate change has never been a change for the better. For the youth, if indulging in drugs is a harmful exercise in futility, physical exercise a productive and positive exercise in pursuit of longevity, emotional and physical stability, self-love and self-worth.

I learn from the young businessman that exercise can break the cycle of worry and distraction, draw tension from the body, and can prevent excessive weight gain, heart diseases and cancers. Therefore, adults should move more and sit less. What message does he have for the person who has been reading the Mohammed Bushera story? "As a young, focused and emerging businessman and a humble and needy physical fitness enthusiast, I would be thankful and joyful if people help me grow my business venture. I wish I could live my entrepreneurial dreams". A spirit of entrepreneurship epitomizes and promises big and bright dreams for the African youth. Entrepreneurship brings about financial freedom and job-creation. The youth are the future. Needless to say that souls who are able and willing to help out in whatever way possible, those who have a big and blessed heart or who are touched by his story, noble efforts, inspiration and vision, kindly call or text him on +251 091 123 2716.

Let us do it in the name of posterity, progress, love, oneness and empathy and in service of humanity. Humanity's honourable dreams can be realized. I believe that we are here on Earth not only to live life to the fullest but also to leave a lovely legacy by making a positive difference to the lives of the needy and the youth. *Let us all strive today in order to thrive tomorrow. For today's miles of efforts can be tomorrow's smiles of success.* **Here's to a happy, healthy, peaceful, positive, productive and poetry-filled 2023!**

That Days General Knowledge Lesson

It was early morning, but already her ship was shaky, awry and unnerving. If anything the first two lessons were a complete mess and a dizzying nightmare for the science teacher who had just got married to another teacher in another nearby school.

The man kept coming for her in spite of her humblest and loudest pleas and protestations. He had his way of clawing and sneaking into her classroom almost on a daily for no other reason than to echo: *I love you.*

She prayed and hoped the third lesson of the day would be better, less chaotic and frustrating— being a General Knowledge one. However, the tricky thing about it was that she was covering for someone else who was on maternity leave, and was least prepared to follow her lesson objectives and steps. She thought about an ideal warmer for an engaging start. Her lesson plan had a short mental discussion about the importance of TV.

Teacher: Who can tell me why he or she takes time to view and listen to the main evening news on TV? What can we learn from the evening bulletins?

Thulani: I hardly take a conscious move to listen to the news on TV. Every day you are likely going to watch and listen to one big bore in the shameless name of our president ,harping on nonexistent growth,peace and unity. Do you think I've peace of mind when I see him on TV talking about these things when my uncle is jobless because his actions and policies weakened and destroyed viable companies? Do you know that my uncle and several innocent souls were tortured and orphaned by Bob's red berated men during a genocide that he later conveniently called a *moment of madness*? Does he talk about it on TV? Do you think he's man and honest enough to discuss it on TV? Then do you think I see him and his colleagues in crime as heroes? Hell no! Bloody villains! On the score of that genocide ,isn't it general knowledge that he is no Pan-Africanist either? I refuse to be deceived by locally published history books which masquerade as text books but portray clearly shameless and one-sided lies and distortions that are not even worth the paper they are written on. Do they teach us about ZAPU's heroic role in the liberation war? Do you know why decent citizens ditched the national TV? *Whoopla*. What we can learn from the main evening news on a daily basis is that someone has so outstayed his welcome and gone past his sell-by date that he cannot even see that he is a narcissistic nuisance, and that my uncle and others want answers. *Justice*.

Sipho: Yes, Bob is a big bore. I'm not surprised that he was a teacher before he clawed his way into the upper echelons of That Days General Knowledge Lesson politics. What a disaster!

Students: Yeah...boring Bob was a teacher!!! (All of them yelling in unison).

Teacher: OK, OK. Calm down! What's his real name? Let's be positive and nice.

Thulani: I don't care what his real name is because the bottom line is that he was a teacher and is a big, big bore. We all know that. How can we be positive and nice when he has done all these negative and mean things? Teacher, get real. Is that too much to ask? I mean, is he not a mean old man? Is he not a big bore?

Sipho: Yes, Bob's a big, big bore. A yelling yawn. I'm not surprised that there's a lot of chaos here. My mom says we are suffering because of his follies and failures. The teacher was a bit frustrated and restless, but she tried to steady herself. *Let me give it another go. Let me breathe life and direction into this lesson.*

Teacher: How do we do our homework assignments in a way that makes us get good scores or comments?

Sethu: By waiting for the teacher to give us answers.

Thulani: No, we let our parents do the stuff for us. They know better.

Sipho : No, our elder brothers and sisters are more knowledgeable. Just hand over the work to them. They will do wonders!

Teacher: Our topic today is TV and its advantages for the learner. What is an *advantage,* anyone?

Sethu: It's a part of our topic.

Teacher: How can we keep order in class, Thulani?

Thulani: keeping away from class. By simply staying at home. That's it!

Teacher: What do you call cockroaches in SiNdebele or in any other language?

Sipho: It's not a good idea to call upon cockroaches, to call them by phone. They just march, invade your kitchen, home without necessarily receiving a friendly phone call in any language under the sun. Damn cockroaches, I'd never call them in any language.

Teacher: Name one nation you don't' particularly like on any continent.

Students: Exami—Nation! PLEASE don't start us on that one!

Teacher: *One day learners will thank teachers for a job well done.* What tense is that?

Thulani: I'm *tense*. I'm anxious to see that day. Unfortunately I won't be among those learners. Tough luck!

Sethu: I think it's called the *future impossible*!

Teacher: *Thulani is coming over to pick up Sethu.* Begin the sentence with Sethu.

Sipho: Sethu, Thulani is coming over to pick you up. By the way teacher, your husband has just come over to say he loves you! Honestly.

The teacher looked out through a window and, there was her sneaking and tiptoeing man. She could not wait to hear those three little words again.

For Everyday Life

Perhaps the expression, *life is what you make it is* still relevant today in spite of some people's personal beliefs which are rooted in the power of fate or destiny rather than in decision or action.

After working for several months or years, sometimes we feel the desire to go on vacation in order to recharge the batteries. One day I made a choice to visit the mighty Victoria Falls, and chose the mode of transport I would use to get to that world-famous tourist centre, also known as the

Adventure Capital of Africa or the Adrenalin Capital of Africa.

The linking buzzword between my choice of destination— southern Africa's safari hub and my choice of transportation is none other than *mathematics.*

I am a teacher by profession and a poet by avocation. As an educator and author, I use my laptop almost on a daily basis for compiling classroom lessons, charts and graphs, for writing and data storage purposes. I consider any working computer as a *mathematical genius.* Teaching has been known to be a noble profession. Like any job, what makes it noble is how one applies mathematics to one's personal and professional schedules. Without that mathematical flair, it can be an ignoble and thankless occupation. Jamie Lyn Beatty Thi is of the opinion that, "Jobs fill your pocket, but adventures fill your soul". Traveling begets memories. No amount of money can buy our recollections of our experiences. We are the best witnesses of our travels and experiences.

A person who hits a jackpot and then goes on a spending spree without accounting for each and every cent is like a businessperson who cannot work out how much he/she needs to charge for his/her services or goods. Evidently, the danger of failing to think logically or mathematically can lead into a disaster no matter how much money one has.

Along the Victoria Falls road, I saw few thriving businesses and farms. I knew that the owners had basic models which detailed their business concepts like procedures, processes, practices, production costs, staff wages, assets and liabilities.

Some shop attendants were doing some stocktaking and bookkeeping. Mathematics was certainly at work.

Of course, I do not need to be a rocket scientist or a mathematician to know that the salary and perks of the job need to be enough to keep the family ship afloat. If it is not enough, mathematics tells me that there is sufficient reason to jump ship job wise. That means that the first port of call before one signs a contract is to examine the overall value of the job. For example, I would do a calculation of my expenses. How much money would go into fundamental bills like rentals, utilities, car insurance, car maintenance, house maintenance, fuel consumption, school fees, life cover and health cover? How much money would I save after paying off these bills?

Would I have enough for capital projects like extending one's residential property or investing for a business venture like a café? Would I have enough money to spoil myself and my family once in a while with outings and gifts or to keep up with technological advances in terms of household gadgets, laptops and mobile phones?

I remember that before I embarked on the trip to the Victoria Falls, which is also known as "Mosi oa-Tunya" ("the smoke that thunders"), I had to consider time and the duration. Would it be a two-day adventure? Would I go there by car or by train or by plane? Being a big fan of safari, I decided to go there between May and October when the vegetation is comparatively low and animals are easily spotted. Of course, this happened after determining figures in terms of the temperature and the best time to visit Victoria Falls, and the specific experiences I sought to invest myself and time in. Being fearful of a night safari, I chose a morning drive, and told myself that next time perhaps I would go for an afternoon one. Some people chose rented bikes or rented cars for touring purposes but I said: canoe and copter take me away. Next time, maybe a horseback expedition.

Why not? The Victoria Falls is not only a World Heritage Site, it is also an incredible adventure travel centre. If *mathematics* is the abstract science of numbers, quantity and space, then *statistics* is the science that deals with the collection, organisation, displaying, analysis, interpretation and presentation of data. Figures feature predominantly in statistics. There is a general belief that figures do not lie and are synonymous with neutrality, evidence and exactness. If statistics are anything to go by, the Falls is one of Africa's paramount, most-loved and most-visited attractions and is considered as one of the world's most striking natural phenomena. For example, Victoria Falls registered over seventeen thousand arrivals just in the first quarter of 2018. Statistically speaking, the Victoria Falls Bungee Jump is consistently considered and selected as one of the top five Adrenalin experiences on the entire planet. It is a sure momentary experience that releases adrenaline into the body. We use mathematics to time experiences. Mathematics always comes in handy. The Victoria Falls Bungee Jump takes four magic seconds of free fall and one hundred and eleven meters of perfect Adrenalin leap in "no man's land". That is awesome. Talk of the Adrenalin rush doing what it knows best—increasing the heart rate and the speed at which the brain works, thereby causing a gush in energy. Talk of an adventurous jump that triggers a fight-or-flight response with a life of its own!

Before arriving in Victoria Falls, I had done my math on things like food and accommodation. I had reminded myself of the fact that Victoria Falls offers countless exciting things. Obviously since I did not have limitless funds and time, I had to choose those activities I could afford. I had an unforgettable time flying above the rare Falls in a helicopter, white waterrafting and going on a sunset river cruise. There is no gainsaying the fact that there is a mathematical formula to all this. There is no aviation or an expedition without figures. The number of people and animals I saw, even the birds and their nests, the insects and their habitations, all exemplified and glorified some mathematical patterns in nature's drapery. Our everyday life is decorated with mathematical decisions and actions.

It is clear that it took some numerical and logical thinking to have such a memorable trip. Needless to say that we need a basic understanding of mathematics in life in order solve some of our challenges or to develop economically and intellectually. Mathematics enables us to make sense of the figures and facts of our dynamic life. Can climate change be effectively addressed without concerted efforts and relevant budgets? No. The number of family members or friends one has, the doctor's prescription, the challenges to sustainable development caused by climate change –all these need mathematical steps to carry out.

Life is a journey, and the places and things we experience are part of that voyage. Saint Augustine once said, "The world is a book, and those who do not travel, read only one page". There are many places we wish we could explore. One of the aspirations on Susan Sontag's wish list was "everywhere". Actually, she put it in a remarkable way like this: "I haven't been everywhere, but it's on my list". Mathematics is a systematic application of matter. If we pay careful attention to it, our lives tend to be methodical. Mathematics is an antithesis of chaos and nondescript elements.

Architectural beauty is synonymous with mathematical clarity. Think about beautifully-designed houses and wellengineered bridges and dams one cannot take one's eyes off. I have had the pleasure of seeing such creations in the Middle East. Mathematics can be viewed as the mother of all creations.

Every day, every activity and every move I undertake is mathematical in nature: from choosing the time to sleep or wake up in the morning, to the steps one takes into the bathroom, the number of cups and teaspoons one takes during tea, to the dress code and colors and departure time one opts for. Every time I travel to a new place, new city or country, I am left amazed and enriched, but most importantly I become the chronicler of my journeys. Ibn Battuta says, "Traveling—it leaves you speechless, then turns you into a storyteller."

Mathematics is more than mere statistics. For it boosts the power of problem-solving, reasoning, and creativity. It is a cradle which houses and nurtures critical thinking, creative thinking and effective communication. On the importance of traveling and exploring the world, Robyn attractively and creatively sums it up like this," We travel not to escape life, but for life not to escape us". Thanks for reading this story, guess what, you really made a good mathematical move!

WEARING THE ATTIRE OF A SKUNK

Indeed as they escorted me to the police station via the fully packed waiting room, there was no gainsaying it.

There was no disputing that people were already putting me on trial. I had become the focal point. I was being slapped with a certain conviction. Common belief is: *a thief is one who has been caught.* In the eyes of some witnesses there is a thin line between a criminal and a suspect. The residents of all ages stared at me. No, the crux of the matter is that the entire world seemed to focus on me. The judgmental world weighed heavily upon me. Its fangs stabbed my heart. My eyes were too heavy to fall on the residents. I could not. Whose eyes can face the rays of the sun? Who can withhold the awesome weight of the multitudes? My sins seemed to be higher than Mount Everest. In the vein of a scoundrel, a rat caught nibbling away little stolen peanuts; I set my quaking eyes on my chained hands. I could feel the residents' gazes: heavy on me, piercing me, prodding me and even probing me. I was averting them but I knew what those stunned looks meant to my image and reputation as the public's trustee. Emotionally, the incident looked set to be with me for the rest of my life. I was drowning in my own cesspool of mortification. Those eyeballs X-rayed my heart down to the very base of the cesspit where, unexpectedly layers and layers of chagrin and chastisement could be could not be ignored or deadened.

I was already tainted. Having suffered such a loss of face, it was no effortless act to just cut a loss. The forefathers believed: *that a mud-covered cow is as good as one that has drunk the water.* It reminded me of the fireplace story of the two messengers: *the Tortoise and the Gecko. The Tortoise is said to have been the bearer of good news and the truth while on the other hand, the Gecko was the messenger who brought bad news and damaging distortions. Tortoise being some kind of foot-dragger or dawdler was outpaced by Gecko who delivered his own twisted and detrimental message to satisfy his own selfish ends. By the time the laggardly -moving tortoise arrived where other animals were, no- one was keen to give him as much as an ear let alone heed his advice. It only dawned upon the animals that Gecko had misrepresented the facts when the bigger damage had been done.*

Solid solitude kept me company: I, the rotten witch. I, the villain. It tickled my ego. Heavily, it sat on my back, weighed on my fate, pricked on my conscience. Beginning to feel sullied and sullen, I was pining for prompt action to wash my hands. It was as if my hands and mouth had been forcefully plunged into a plate full of sewage itself, and my entire body was laying a charge of crimen injuria against the perpetrators of that dastardly act. There was a leprous air about my presence that cried out for a clean-up act. A cleansing ritual. A transforming bath. It was as if I had been doused with intense soot and painted yellow with exceedingly fetid human excrement. There was an olfactory touch to it. The unbearable stench of a skunk haunted and hurt me. I could feel it on my mind and breath, and even picture it all over my body. It became me. It drugged me, dragged me into mud and mess, mental disruptions and revulsions. It was fast melting away my humanity. Rancid and reprehensible. Rubbing off on my innocent parents. Normally, every parent wishes the best in life for their child. No normal parent wants to bad-mouth their children. It is always a parent's ardent desire to see the child not only succeed in life but also becoming a pillar of virtue and vision, the pride of the family, not a monument of blight, disarray and vice.

A single detention for me was as bad as one too many. It meant a life of mess, dilemmas, afflictions, and foolery. The question of my detention kept on making a dramatic return to the mental discourse of my plight. How was l to fumigate the plague of dishonour visited on my reputation, a development that held my peace and sense of humanness in captive and in the balance? How were l to admonish my future offspring and grandchildren about shying away from crime and detention? My detestation's of crimes and injustices of any nature were my nature. I had been schooled in the philosophy that screamed that a cow that has trod upon muddy territories cannot moo of thirst and expect to draw sympathy and attention. I was an adherent of such thinking. A disciple of crime-free living principles. My feet were muddy. It was reminiscent of a scenario in which a young man denied being responsible for the pregnancy of a young woman in the village. The elders hearing and handling the case would pose one critical question: *Do you know the girl?* If the answer was in the affirmative, the young man would summarily be told in no uncertain terms that he had wasted the elderly jury's precious time and hence should just stop whimpering and denying and foot the manly bill of his sweat in silence and with dignity. It reminded one of a didactic traditional song*: one who has hit a bird has not eaten it. He who has eaten the bird has actually eaten the crime*. I felt like one whose dignity had been indelibly eroded. How could l say l like the meat but hate the gravy that is derived from the same beef? How can one behave like misogynists who loathe the Eves of this world yet all of them are born of women? How could l say l want the groundnut plant and at the same time claim to dislike the nuts? If one wants to marry a woman with two children, how could they say they love the mother minus her offspring? Is it not disingenuous to pour scorn on the well, and speaking glowingly about the water drawn from such a repository? On that front, l had failed my parents as well. I felt that way. The tag of failure exerted a strain on my scruples.

A netted fish, l was. I felt like an ensnared mammal, one trapped by the trappings of man's pride and power. It curiously looked fishy. Upon arriving at the station, the police officers who had brought me in seemed to have other fish to dry and fry. No, they had not brought me in. They had dumped me in a thudding manner. Quarantined me. No, they had not forgotten about me. They had done their mandate. Had they not arrested me as planned? For more than two hours l was stuck on a bench like an intractable blood-sucking tick on a cow's tail. I did not expect them to treat me with kid gloves, or treat me like a fragile egg or a high and mighty king. Even at a tender age, I had not grown under mollycoddling parental care. Occasionally, I received cuddles and praises. They cared not so much as to tolerate or turn me into a spoilt brute. I knew better than to be mired in delinquent antics. In fact, they had been disciplinarians in their own right. Neither did l look forward to receiving some far-fetched miraculous ministrations like a natural disaster victim in dire need of medical care. I was not going to cry mawkishly over their shoulders," Look, caring people, please throw my case out of the roof on health grounds, I'm battling with smallpox and a stubborn headache." *A man does not cry, his tears trickle not beyond the chest area.*

I was pensive, with many different ideas, now and then flooding my mind like different posts popping up in one's news feed on a social networking site. Now it was my mother's visit from our rural place, my wife and her pregnancy; then the thought process took me on a journey to the occasional meetings and key responsibilities as ward spokesman, to the scathing letter l had written to a newspaper editor after an anonymous person had twisted all the facts and figures in my guest writer column, the thought and time that went into the crafting of that article; the general degeneration and frustration of life, the blatant lies and hypocrisy, the syndrome of sweeping rot under the carpet, the hard-to-come promotion, nepotism and other horrible isms, corruption, the weekend activities, the Monday and its issues and tissues. My happy visits to the two old suburbs of Gug'uzukhokhobe and Hlab'umxhwele and shifting blame: l failed you instead of admitting that one failed. *Through our decisions, we make or mar our lives.*

I gained an insight into the hypocrisy of shielding oneself behind a finger. I was lost in thought. I thought of social and political job offers l had rebuffed for one reason or the other. I was not sure whether or not it was with regret or contentment that I had seen those offers or opportunities go begging. Do people not sometimes conclude, after failing or making conspicuously wrong decisions that everything happens for a reason? Not a convenient excuse for our failures and shortcomings of judgment in life! On a lighter note, l reflected on the music that was my pleasure. My mind wondered to the treasure of books l ferreted for time and again, day and night. I mean the ones that intrigued my mind to caress, kiss and make passionate love to them. I contended that a world devoid of the beauty and power of the written word was a hollow, loveless and meaningless hole. I found books to be revelatory and transformational. The word enabled me to feel, touch, see, listen to and speak with the world. I was the interviewer and the world was the interviewee. I knew that a chatty interviewer could learn but little while vocalizing. Hence my pen does the talking for the society. It keeps at bay humdrum things and characters. It does the walking for me, for it is my walking stick. It does the recording and reading from the stage. That is my writing feather's mandate. True, the moment l penned my first story many, many years ago, the tone was set. Certainly the stage was set, the horizon was illuminated. I wanted to galvanize words into action, written expressions to breathe hope into a seemingly hopeless situation, utterances to scream bitter truth in the face of sweet hypocrisy. In fact, an indelible embryonic link between me and the written word was established .l was reborn. A relationship whose only possible divorce, no matter the nature and storminess of the currents and challenges- is the afterlife: if it would have nothing to do with sedentary and literary careers!

The wafting and soothing magic of the world of music set my heart alight, brightened up my vision and healed my head. The awesomeness of God was manifest in the creators of such melodies and stimulating sets of printed sheets of paper. *Mundane life is a form of detention.* Though l was in a detention centre, my mind was wild, wide and free. It brooked no detention, definition, no sacrosanct and frippery physical decorations and limitations. It knew no sacred cows. It broke down walls of confinement. It knew no physical boundary. I pictured myself scribbling away with a hungry fury. I could mentally read some of the salient lines: *The storm will be over. Determine your destiny. Just steady yourself, persevere, push forward, focus on what you want, sooner or later you will reach your destination and claim what is yours.*

I could crawl out of any slave centre without as much as an escape route. Spiritually, and mentally, l crawled out of my detained body. I was at liberty to look back and forth. I flew high and low, turned ideas over and under, constructed my world, destroyed it with speed only to recreate another and yet another. I was retracing footsteps, clamouring for a modicum of a meaning of life. Hence I was reciting a miniature portion of life, seeking to determine a destiny. I was thus miniaturizing my life like a technologised world to today's globe. My mind was running amok. The world was wild and weird. Its turns and twists were sometimes evasive and elusive.

My brainpower went on, probing, purging and perfecting. I had a craving for something. I yearned to drink from that pool. The pool that widens thinking, that illuminates one's character and broadens one's horizon. That puddle of knowledge, that pond of education, that funny fooling fountain of understanding and ideas. Yes, l just had a hankering to douse my head a little. I had seen them. Others had done it to a certain extent. I could. One. Yes, be that as it may, everything starts and ends with the trio, the pivotal three committee m embers: *the vision, the mind and the heart*. I saw it, the mind consulted the endorsing committee member: heart, and a decision was thus reached.

It was around 11:15 am. Akin to the tendencies and conduct of some social misfits and misanthropists, it dawned on me that I was being avoided. It was as if the mere act of entering the station had phenomenally metamorphosed me into a leper to be quarantined, come rainstorm, come hell fire. Where were the accusers? So they have indeed swooped upon me? What a "raid"? International criminals on the loose, those who have committed crimes against humanity are issued with warrants of arrests? So am I a criminal of sorts as well? Thoughts, thoughts, and questions -all were racing on my mind. I was turning them over, chewing them on my mind.

Save Our Nation

As the nation continued to sink deeper and deeper into serious political and economic challenges, I remember my friend inviting me to a seminar on "Changing Values and Beliefs to Save our Nation".

One leadership expert bemoaned the woeful behaviours of government officials, company managers and executives and senior management of loss-making parastatals and other state institutions. Specifically citing the problems bedeviling the power utility, she predicted an even bleaker future for the nation if corrective action was not taken immediately. She spoke of the lack of courage in having a measure of proactive ownership of the electricity challenges related to corruption, debt, salaries, perks, prices and inefficient use; saying that the country was on the throes of singing the blues of blackouts and resultant mass disinvestments and alarming economic collapse. She reiterated that there was no option but to work on a drive to invest in energy-efficient methods and processes. She stated that it was baffling and sickening that government officials sacrificed national interests to please the hugely corrupt state agencies' executives and ruling party's loyalists who were "swimming in a pool of stinking wealth" in the midst of abject poverty affecting the generality of the country's workers.

Another speaker said amid cases of high-level corruption one was bound to ask where that decay of behaviours was going to lead Msindazwe to if not arrested. He declared, "Such undesirable behaviours are not only worrisome but also the tip of the iceberg, and a symptom of a broader decadent system. There is an urgent need for a culture shift that would radically and collectively address and respond to the questions of profound personal values and beliefs of the entire leadership and communities. This country, mark my words, is on a dangerous slope, on the brink of tottering on its last legs. There has to be a paradigm shift. The giant is on the verge of slumping into an economic slumber. It is faced with some sort of demise. We have to revitalize it. We do not oppose any indigenisation law that empowers the people. We need to have cool heads, otherwise food security will be compromised. Land was stolen. Land is their birthright. Deuteronomy 16: 20 reads, '"Follow justice and justice alone, so that you may live and process the land the Lord your God is giving you." If the ruling elitists are helping themselves to a multiplicity of farms, at the expense of the poor and landless, is that justice? We have to put the people at the centre of our policies. It should be within the realms of our imagination to ensure that the past social inequalities are rigorously addressed. We have to act with care, otherwise such an indigenisation drive can turn out to be the people's worst enemy as companies flounder and disappear. Now. Superficial changes will not rescue us.

"'Renaming suburbs like Mjondolo and Amadumba is good but without improving the lives of the relevant residents who live in these places, this will not help anyone. Naming big roads after dubious heroes without taking care of the road networks or upgrading buildings is a farce. Razing down poor people's shacks without providing them with alternative better accommodation is a silly and cynical perpetuation of vagrancy, harassment and pauperisation. It can only win favour perhaps in Hell where torment is the order of things. Not in our country. Forget. Pragmatic leadership is the result, application and separation of good principles and values. We become what we repetitively keep on doing. Repetition of good practices is a core element in the development of character, values and actions. I leave you with one question: Where are the seamless leaders who will lead and enable this wonderful nation to reach her full potential?"

He posed three major questions. "The starting point is prognosis. Therefore, the way forward is to ask ourselves: exactly what are the entrenched personal values and beliefs of leaders and everyone else? Secondly, what collective, positive, and for that matter, negative values and beliefs are being exhibited in the behaviours of the rulers and the ruled? Thirdly, let us look ourselves in the eye in an honest and open way and find out whether we have positive or desirable values and beliefs we are prepared to take as our undeniably collective colossal onus of laying of a foundation and mechanisms for inculcating those desirable values and beliefs into society and organizations? Are we ready to go the route of eliminating values, beliefs and behaviours that stifle the growth of our organizations and the nation? Let me warn you, at leadership level this must not be implemented under the aegis of spineless cronyism. For it calls for great courage, insight, seamless vision and conscious effort to infuse and internalize the desired values and beliefs. Leadership that is based on delivering good speech after the other but lacks action is not good enough for sustainability like a paper-fueled fire. Such leadership ceases to be relevant because it melts with its sugar-coated words. If we don't get our act right now, we will surely slide into an economic coma. Economic recovery can prove elusive and slippery if we bury our heads in the soil like a bunch of hypocritical ostriches. We're our own enemies. We're our own saviours, too. Let us save ourselves now, let us save our nation from further descent into misery and confusion".

I thought of the complicity of the police force in the rot. The role they played in perpetuation of injustices against the citizens. My former teacher's words re-echoed: *The restlessness of some people in the face of a problem sometimes becomes a part of the problem rather than the solution.* One speaker, whose speech was titled, *A Vision Lost is A People Perished*, told the delegates that grievances were simmering under the surface in the companies. And that sooner rather than later they would erupt with dire consequences. She said that politics was intimately related to economics. She also stated that though work on its own was a necessary drudgery, people needed jobs. They could not divorce themselves from fiscal dynamics visited upon by politicians.

"Whether you are a religious person or self-employed person the price of bread you eat, the clothes you wear, the kind of tax you pay, and transport you use is part and parcel of a political game. It is my considered view that no citizen can honestly say: l won't vote because, l am no politician. If you are told lies every week, or told to tighten up your belt every day, or encouraged to do some gymnastics in the face of hunger, and you accept uncritically, then you also lack vision. You will tighten up your belt until the waist is no more! Vision represents the desired future of a people. Without vision, the people perish, even the Bible affirms. A vision serves as a concrete foundation for the organization. For example, where there is no succession plan there is no vision to ensure a suitable supply of successors for present and superior positions arising from business strategy. If the current strategic manager suddenly dies or leaves for one reason or nothing, transition becomes unpredictable at best and disastrous at worst. Can we talk of a vision where corrupt practices are aligned to organizational culture?"

"Daydreaming is not a vision. How can a select few who daydream, line their pockets, then expect others to have a vivid picture of their hallucinations, and even go further to encourage them to feel that their lives and work are intertwined and moving toward such unrecognizable and illegitimate delusions? A credible vision seeks the engagement of all stakeholders, and it becomes an integral part of every employee".

Frustrations in the police force were really raging, manifesting themselves in or culminating in brutality and a general unnerving lack of professionalism. The police commissioners could not care less about the plight of their subordinates, like dishonest army generals who tell their troops not to bring their problems. These are the types of officers whose ostrich mentality deludes them to think that if the troops do not bring their grievances to them then there is no trouble. Professionalism was on the wane for a multitude of reasons, and being used or abused as pawns of oppression and suppression was one of them. They had ceased to carry out their duties as non-partisan public servants. It was not uncommon to hear that, fortunately but rarely some police officers had been caught on the wrong side of the law. Some residents even joked that the traffic officers on the road had palms which itched each time a vehicle appeared, they believed in receiving a gift if not money. I was wondering: Maybe these people are under the influence of some funny substance? *Isihlahla*? (Ganja plant?)Have they not resorted to a drug? And are they not now flying and swimming in their hallucinations? Are they not having itching palms, palms that heal and survive on greasing? Are they not up to some brutal blackmailing mischief? Are they not the crop of pawns that fawns madly in front of their masters as would do obsequious dogs upon the arrival of their owners?

Could it be those unknown male stalkers who remarked at Sindemlonyeni Wengwenya booksellers, "So, I'm a writer?" I was undaunted, and no beads of sweat broke out on my brow as the possibility of their target for shadowing dawned me, or so l told my friend who had asked whether l had fainted or was agitated. Could it be those who traveled undercover and visited my place of residence and purported to be carrying out a national census- which turned out to be a dubious surveillance or something because the neighbours were not visited or counted, neither was the "'national'" exercise publicized! How national can things be here?

By 5pm, the foursome who had arrested me were gone. They were possibly in the comfort of their homes or whiling away time with friends and relatives in a restful and fruitful manner. Yet there languishing, l was. There was no point in shouting and throwing tantrums. From the time the police blitzed on me, little did l know that l was observing a countdown to my own embarrassing drama! Time was staging one upset after the other against me. If it were a football match then mine would have gone into extra or added time. The game had failed to be won or concluded during the regulation time. I was not cherishing that. My game was not up. I had given one of the "'dutiful crew members'" my home phone numbers, because he looked somehow the kindliest of the quartet.

I prayed that it was not going to be a futile case similar to a situation where one person, Mabanjiswilitshe is asked to hold fort, especially a cumbersome boulder only to discover that the soul that one is in lieu of is gone, and gone forever. I did not want to belong to the "'Mabanjiswilitshes of this world'". In desperate situations, some people who are addicted to cunning antics or mere redundant hoodwinking tend to give one desperate victim fake or toy parachutes in the name of rescuing. I hoped he would live up to his words, and inform my immediate family members of the unforeseen arrest. I was not interested in duping games. Enough tricks had already been played on me.

Darkness was slowly setting in - as fate would have it- when an "'owlish'" police threw his weight of inflated, undeserved supremacy about. He told me in no uncertain terms that he was intent upon "fixing me". *Why don't you advise your government to fix poverty which is prospering every single day instead?* I wondered. I asked for his force number and he gave me with a brag, "There's utterly nothing you can do with it!"

If justice were not remote, I would have told him how indefensible his assertion was. But that was an innermost microcosm of the crisis. Some people trampled on the rights of others with impunity because they enjoyed dubious immunities which added no amenities to their communities. Justice was languishing. It was miserably rotting in the intensive care unit.

Roaring Into Bulawayo's Royal Treat

It was an inspiring cool August afternoon when the Boeing 767 carrying Ahmed landed majestically in the center of the Joshua Mqabuko Nkomo International Airport runway, 25 km to the north of Bulawayo. That Friday I was glad that Ahmed, my former student from Kuwait, had finally arrived in Bulawayo. After exchanging some warm and excited greetings, he remarked," "Beautiful airport. I like it!" I smiled, "Though small in size, it is our gateway to such amazing world heritage sites as the Khami Ruins and the Matobo Hills".

When we arrived home, I gave him a bit of background information about Bulawayo. "This city was founded by none other Lobengula, the Ndebele king who was a son to King Mzilikazi. Born of Matshobana, he settled in contemporary Zimbabwe around the 1840s after the Ndebeles' great march from Nguniland. As the second largest city in Zimbabwe, Bulawayo has more than two nicknames. One famous one is 'Ntuthu ziyathunqa' — which is a Ndebele phrase for 'a place where smoke guts out '. Historically, Bulawayo was the country's massive industrial base, and even today one can see gigantic cooling towers of the coal-powered electricity generating plant in the city centre. In the olden days these towers used to emit steam and smoke all over the place. Bulawayo is affectionately known as the City of Kings and Queens." Ahmed interjected with a joke, "I'd like to be an heir to the throne too. This royal city has good quality tap water."

I disclosed to him that not only does Bulawayo boast of pumping and maintaining the healthiest and tastiest quality tap water in the country, furthermore, it has been widely acknowledged as the cleanest and best-managed city in Zimbabwe. With one of the friendliest and humblest African citizens on the continent, the respect for visitors and all is a cultural protocol and pleasure for the locals. There are no major security concerns as the street crime levels are largely low and isolated. In spite of the country-wide economic challenges, the metropolitan's cultural richness and service delivery to the generality of the residents and tourists is second to none. "It hardly recycles waste water. It uses treated waste water for irrigation purposes. As an integral, industrial, cultural and logistical hub, the city was known to provide rail links between Botswana, South Africa, and Zambia".

Knowing that he loves soccer and cricket, I decided to give him a dose of sport update. I touched on local soccer teams and the current log standings, including the best-performing local cricketers in particular and the level and spirit of national cricket in general. "By the way, Bulawayo is home to the Queens Sports Club and Bulawayo Athletic Club, just two of the three pitches in Zimbabwe where test match cricket has been played. Additionally, it is home to Hartsfield on which a number of Southern Africa's prominent rugby players have Roaring Into Bulawayo's Royal Treat participated. It is home to one of Zimbabwe's greatest sports persons of all time: international soccer prodigy Peter "Nsukuzonke" Ndlovu. The city has an undeniable unstoppable history and pedigree of unleashing greatness upon greatness on the arena of leisure and entertainment. Big names like those of Heath Streak and Henry Khaaba Olonga easily come to the fore, just to name a few, and there is no pun intended here! Henry Olonga was the first black cricket player and the youngest-ever player to represent Zimbabwe at international level".

We also touched on the importance of conserving Africa's precious resources in terms of the land in spite of mining activities. I bemoaned the illegal mining activities that were taking place in the villages which are a cause for concern as they result in land degradation, soil erosion and deaths of both animals and people. We talked about the climate change crisis and its adverse effects of several droughts and heat waves and floods.

* * *

On Saturday morning we cruised all the way to the Natural Museum of Zimbabwe which is situated in the Centenary Park in Bulawayo. Built in 1962, with its spectacular exhibitions and precious research collections, it is the finest arts center in Southern Africa and rated fourth in magnitude among the museums of Africa. I watched Ahmed as his eyes were fixed on the public display galleries, the beauty of the lecture hall, the study collections, the artifacts, the well-preserved animals in the displays. "Your eyes are fixed on the displays", I said. He chuckled," Fixed...actually my eyes are feasting on these attractive and informative displays here. I'm awed by the magnificence and abundance of one of the best natural history museums in the world".

Ahmed's itinerary glimmered with mouth-watering names like the Khami Ruins, Bulawayo Railway Museum, Chipangali Wildlife Orphanage and Research Centre, Bulawayo National Gallery of Zimbabwe, The Hillside Dams Conservancy, Tshabalala Game Sanctuary, Old Bulawayo and Mzilikazi Art and the Craft center. I admired his travel programme. However, I thought it lacked one three-word ingredient to consummate a regal experience: Matobo National Park! I did not have to convince him because on Monday we drove toward the black eagles, the black and white rhinos and the scenic balancing rock formations in the heart of Matobo National Park. *Ahmed was speechless.*

ABOUT THE AUTHOR

Sibanda is a Bulawayo-born poet, novelist, and nonfiction writer who has a passion for themes and topics around conservation, nature, development and justice. He believes that he is a poet in prose, and hence he has never looked back since building and marching into the very first poetry pharmacy in the world, where poetry ... and poetry and poetics are the most tonic threesome prescriptions.

We Are Not An Error But The Idioms Of Our Era brings Ndaba's tally of published books to thirty. He has coauthored more than 100 published books and several peer- reviewed articles.

Sibanda has received the following nominations: the National Arts Merit Awards (NAMA), the Mary Ballard Poetry Chapbook Prize, the Best of the Net Prose and the Pushcart Prize. Sibanda's book *Notes, Themes, Things And Other Things: Confronting Controversies ,Contradictions And Indoctrinations* was considered for *The 2019 Restless Book Prize for New Immigrant Writing in Nonfiction.* Ndaba's book titled *Cabinet Meetings: Of Big And Small Preys* was considered for *The Graywolf Press Africa Prize 2018.* Sibanda is a three-time Pushcart nominee. He can be spotted landscaping, lurking, lounging and even lost on various and many media networks.